Christine L[?]

Armstrong

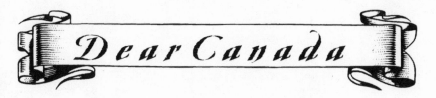

Footsteps in the Snow

The Red River Diary of Isobel Scott

BY CAROL MATAS

Scholastic Canada Ltd.

Aboard the *Prince of Wales*, bound for Rupert's Land, July, 1815

Mother is dead.

As I write in these pages for the first time I worry that I will be left with nothing but smudges and ink blots if I cannot stop my tears.

As Father and I were going through Mother's trunk to find a dress to bury her in, this diary fell out from the folds of her grey silk — her very best frock. I picked it up and handed it to Father.

He read the opening page, all Mother had a chance to write. Before I could stop him, he ripped the page out, crumpled it and tossed it to the floor. Then he threw the diary into the corner of the room. I hurried over and retrieved it and picked up the single sheet as well. "I'll take the diary, Father. I'll carry it on for her." Father didn't seem to hear me. But somehow I thought that if I could save the diary, I could save part of Mother.

As I write that here it almost sounds foolish, but I do not think either of us was thinking clearly at that moment. I do believe, however, that this can be a way for me to talk to Mother, so I will write of our journey in these pages.

Here is what Mother had written. I copy it for posterity:

I begin with such hope in my heart. Within the week we will be sailing over the great sea. I will be gazing toward the New World, gulls swooping overhead, my heart soaring with them because I know we go to a land that is vast and noble, a land where we will once again be proud and be able to stand tall.

We did bury her in the grey silk. I remember the stories she told me about that dress — how she had worn it on festive evenings when her father would entertain the neighbours in their grand house. I can imagine her now — red hair close about her face, blue eyes shining and her mouth always curled up as if she were laughing at some private joke, the ballroom bright with the light of chandeliers, the orchestra playing, and Mother the delight of all.

But what a terrible writer I am! I just realized that I have not mentioned that I am writing this from a ship called the *Prince of Wales*. And I have not even noted the date and the time. In fact, I am not sure what the exact date is. I will ask one of the sailors and put it in the next time. I promise I will try to improve, as Mother would expect me to do my best.

Robbie is lost without Mother. At nine years he is old enough to accept that she will never return, but not old enough to understand it. Mind you, I'm not sure any of us understands. James, being such a good older brother, tries to cheer him with his never-ending wit and humour, but all his attempts seem to fall flat. The companionship Robbie normally shares with Father is also taken from him, as Father is too sunk in grief to notice anything.

Father sits listlessly on his bunk all day. I have to practically drag him up on deck. He speaks to no one.

I remember the day, just after my twelfth birthday, when Father came home looking fit to burst, with the news that would change our lives forever. A more different man than the one I see before me I cannot imagine. His eyes shone with excitement. He could barely stand still. "I have met with a fellow who represents the Earl of Selkirk," he said. "He is recruiting men to leave Scotland to settle in Rupert's Land in the New World! It will mean a long sea voyage. But in the New World we will own our own land. And the Red River, apparently, is in a fertile valley, with a growing season long enough to bring in a good crop. This is our chance," Father had declared. "This is our chance to make something of ourselves. To start over. To become landowners. To rise in the world. And not always live in servitude."

Mother had laughed with delight. "You need not convince me, William," she said. "We will go on the biggest adventure of our lives." At that she tossed the sewing that was in her hands up in the air and Father caught her in his arms and they spun around and around as if they could hear the music and they were dancing in a ballroom filled with candles and flowers.

I pictured us living in a grand house in the New World, with servants to wait on me and young men coming to call. I wasn't frightened, not at all. Of course, I was sorry to think of leaving my friends, but in a way I had known all along, my whole life, that I would be leaving. I was destined for a better life. And now it was coming true.

July 17

Today I spent some time sewing, altering some of Mother's dresses so they would fit me. Father came across me doing so. He lifted the sleeve of one dress, dropped it and then finally spoke. "Have I told you, Isobel, how your mother and I met?"

I have heard it numerous times, of course, but was so happy to hear Father speak at all, I simply said, "Please tell me, Father." I put down my sewing and waited while he settled himself beside me.

"When your mother was only eighteen, her father lost all his money on some scheme he had invested in. Your mother, along with her three sisters, was forced to find employment. And in a way that was a lucky day for me, because she became a governess in a big house in the south of Scotland, where I was working in the stables taking care of the racehorses.

"I fell in love with her the moment I saw her, and she loved me too. But we could not marry, being of such different stations. We would meet secretly when the family went away and we could walk together and talk. Finally we decided to run away. I remember that day. It was cold and a hard rain fell, but we felt like it was the sunniest day there had ever been. We . . . " Here his voice trailed off.

"What then, Father?" I urged him, even though I could have recited the story myself almost word for word. I wanted to keep him talking, hoping that it would help his grief. And also, I must admit, just to be with him. I feel so lonely without Mother, and now, in a way, without him.

"We rented land in the Highlands, but we always had bigger dreams. We imagined owning our own land, giving you children a better life. That's why Mother insisted that you speak English at home, not Gaelic. That's also why she taught you all that fancy needlework."

"And how to pour tea like a lady, and how to walk straight and tall as if balancing a book on the top of my head," I added.

He nodded and then without another word got up and wandered off, seeming to forget all about me again.

July 25

We have sailed past Greenland and are heading into The Davis Strait. Two of the sailors have scrambled into the crow's-nest and are using spyglasses to look for icebergs. This afternoon they spotted whales, and all the young people crowded the railings to get a good view. What a magnificent sight it was, seeing the huge beasts break through the water and then crash back in again, tails slamming the surface, sending waves and spray every which way.

July 27

This morning I taught the Bible class, as Mr. McBeth has become ill. Apparently the adults are unhappy with his tutoring and have asked young John Matheson to take his place, which he will do tomorrow. Then classes will be held regularly from 11 until 2 daily. I have been asked to be an assistant, since my English is so advanced compared to the rudimentary English of most of the others on the ship.

I read from Exodus. And I could not help but think of Mother, who will never reach the Promised Land, just as Moses was kept away by God himself.

She was so excited as we packed. She couldn't wait to go on such an adventure. And she cared little about leaving things behind. She did take the good silver that she had been given from her father's estate when it was liquidated, but only in case we needed to sell it at some point. Other than that it was all practicality. We packed our warm clothes, shawls, stockings, gloves and sturdy boots. "It will be a hard life at first," she warned me. "Hard, backbreaking work. Don't be dreaming of servants and an easy life, my little Isobel. Be prepared for what will come. It may be your children who will see the easy life, not you at all. Remember, we will not own the land right away; we will have to work for it."

"I know that, Mother," I assured her.

"The Hudson's Bay Company has granted this land to Lord Selkirk and your father says that it is not to be all smooth sailing. They are a fur trading company, and already a rival fur trading company — The North West Company — has been sending men to discourage us from sailing. They warn of all sorts of trials in Rupert's Land."

"I don't give a trifle for that," I scoffed. "One day we will own our own land. And then we can build a grand estate, the envy of everyone."

At the same time, I was sorry to say good-bye to Helen — it is hard to part from your dearest friend since childhood. There is talk that soon everyone in the Highlands will have to leave because the land is to be given over to the sheep. But that has not happened yet in our area, and we hope for the sake of the people we are leaving behind that it will not.

Just when I think I am getting better, I find myself suddenly and unexpectedly weeping. I try to find a private place because I don't want to worry James or Robbie. However, James discovered me this morning, huddled in a corner, and tried to cheer me up. The boat was rolling quite a bit — the wind was up.

He said, "Do you know what I tell anyone who is feeling seasick? I tell them to put a coin in their teeth before they lean over the side. If that doesn't prevent them from being sick, I'm not sure what will!"

I smiled a little through my tears.

"I know you miss Mother something terrible," James said, patting my hand. "I do too. But she would want us to be happy."

"To be sure, she would," I agreed. "It isn't easy, though."

"McTavish broke his arm," James said, with that serious look on his face that meant he was about to tell another joke.

"Did he?" I said, trying to get into the spirit.

"Oh yes, and he was distraught. Terribly upset. He said to the doctor, 'Doctor, will I be able to play the bagpipes after my arm has mended?' 'Of

course you will, man,' the doctor snapped.
'Really? Isn't that amazing,' McTavish marvelled,
'since I couldn't play them before!'"

I couldn't help but laugh at the silliness of the
joke. James felt he'd done his duty and went in
search of Robbie.

August 1

The ship is navigating through ice fields and
the boat lurches from one mountain of ice to the
next, the sailors pushing it with their long poles
and every once in a while the bottom of the boat
making a dreadful sound as it hits the solid ice
below.

I have made an unpleasant discovery. The
longer we are on board the more closed in I
begin to feel. I have never experienced this feeling before. Of course I have never been closed in
before. It's true that our little house in the hills
was small, but I always knew that if I felt shut in,
which I often did, I could simply go for a long
walk, something I did in all weather. I would
breathe deep of the smells, flowers and trees, and
sometimes I would run, just to feel the wind
against my face. I often stand on deck so I can
feel the wind, but as I look about me all I see is

the great ocean, and right now the ice, and I know I am trapped on this small ship. I must not dwell on these feelings because that will only make things worse.

August 5

We are held fast by the ice. As we settlers have been put in cramped bunks in the forward hold — a dank, dark and cold place I have come to dread — we are trying to spend as little time as possible down there. I have organized games for the children to keep them busy when we are not studying. We play hide-and-seek, of course, and that is by far the most popular game with the young ones. We also play hopscotch and marbles. And we play a game called tippy fingers. I taught them to play it using Robbie the first time: He stands with eyes closed, and hands behind his back. Then another child touches Robbie's finger with his own. Robbie has to guess which child it was and then say how far the child must run. The first time he did it he said ten times around the deck. But Robbie guessed wrong, which meant he needed to run the ten times himself! The children loved it, and it certainly kept my mind off my feelings of discomfort.

Robbie has been very naughty. He was playing near the fishing equipment and I insisted he stop. I couldn't help but worry that he might cut himself on one of the sharp edges. He says he needn't listen to me and that God is bad, so he shall be bad too. I don't know how to answer him.

Is life here on earth really good? Mother always said, "God is good, kind and loving." If that is so, why has God taken Mother away from us? Would not a good, kind and loving God want a mother to stay with her children? Just to think this might be blasphemous, and yet how can one explain such pain?

And it was such a silly thing that took Mother from us. We were in Helmsdale, ready to embark on our voyage, and suddenly with no warning she became ill. The doctor in Helmsdale told us that her blood had become infected from a cut — we all remembered that she had cut herself on the trunk as we were packing, days earlier — and there was nothing he could do for her. I nursed her and tried to cool her fever, but it was fruitless. She told us that we must go to the New Land even if she could not. She said that she was going to a better place where she would dance with the angels until Father came to claim her, and that we too must carry on to our better place. And then she died.

So, naturally, I worry over Robbie and try to keep him from any harm at all.

August 14

Jasper McKay is playing his bagpipes and some of the men and women are dancing. I cannot. I remember he played his pipes as we left the port of Stromness, where we had travelled after Mother's death. The mournful sound of the pipes went right to my heart and I felt I was leaving Mother behind, as well as the country that had been as a mother to me.

August 15

We are finally free of the ice! My feelings of being shut up have been getting worse and worse until I was beginning to fear I could not bear another day. And, of course, the longer we were stuck the longer the voyage would be.

As the time dragged on, I became more and more aware of the other settlers — one in particular who is past annoying, Kate McGilvery. I have not mentioned her or written about her before in these pages, but I suppose I can talk or write about anything in this private book. She is hardly worth a mention, except for the fact that she seems to think I somehow put myself above all others. It is most annoying. She has taken to calling me The Princess or Your Highness. I cannot help the fact that I hold myself well, that my dresses are well-made, that I speak English as well as Gaelic. She is a short, thin thing with dark eyes and dark hair — quite different from me, with my height, my hazel eyes and my reddish hair. She is eleven years old, just a year younger than I am.

Well, I must admit that she got the better of me one day when I let her goad me into a rash act. We were drifting by a huge iceberg, an iceberg so big that many of the men travelled from our ship onto it. First they attached it to the ship with hooks and after that went to collect fresh water. "I dare you, Little Princess," Kate said to me. "I dare you to go across."

All the other children stared.

"I am not frightened," I said, "of anything."

The sailors had descended to the iceberg by rope ladders. Quickly, before anybody could say anything, I leapt onto the ladder and dropped myself onto the iceberg. And I was so thrilled with my daring and with the expressions on their faces that I began to dance and skip and generally show off. Plus it was wonderful to be off the confines of the ship, if only for a few moments. I felt quite giddy — until I realized that most of the sailors had all climbed back up the ladder. One of the last ones to ascend grabbed me in a very unceremonious way and pushed me up the ladder. Fortunately Father saw none of this.

Still, I am not sorry that little Miss Annoyance should see that there is nothing she can scare me with. But for some reason my actions, instead of stopping her fascination with me, seem to have encouraged her. Everywhere I turn there she is, always with an irritating word. It seems no matter what I say, she implies that I am putting on airs, even if it is just to say hello or good morning. "Ooh, doesn't she speak fine!" Kate crows.

"I merely said hello," I retort.

"Merely," she says, eyes rolling upwards. "Merely."

As if uttering that word alone is some sort of crime.

August 17

We are entering Hudson Bay. We get closer to land every second!

August 18

Kate has begun to keep a close eye on the burgeoning romances that seem to be developing between the single men and women on the boat. Anne McKim is the plainest young woman I have ever seen, but a gentle spirit with pleasing manners. She is the eldest of five, and lately Nichol Johnston, a fellow whose pitch-black hair sticks straight up as if he'd just had a terrible fright, has been following her around like a puppy. Kate is never far behind them, taunting under her breath with rhymes like: "Roses are red, violets are blue, the waves crash about us, and I love you." She is merciless in her teasing and the poor young couples can find no peace from her.

August 24

We have just survived the most dreadful storm. I could not write, as we were trapped in the hold as the ship pitched and rolled in the most terrifying way. Robbie was horribly sick, as were many others, and the smell became so bad that others became sick too, until the entire hold smelled of vomit and sweat, and that smell was enough to make the rest of us sick, as well. When the storm was finally over we had to clean up the mess. And every minute I became more and more aware of how close the quarters are until at times I felt I would certainly faint. I refused to allow that to happen; it would have given Kate too many opportunities to torment me.

I am exhausted.

August 27

We have anchored at the mouth of the Nelson River. Father says we are only 20 miles from the Hudson's Bay Company post called York Factory. It is on another river — the Hayes River — that also flows into Hudson Bay. A schooner will come to take us there. The ship's cannon is firing as I write, to let them know that we have arrived. My heart is fluttering like a newborn chick getting ready to be pushed from the nest. I cannot wait to set foot on land, and yet I am nervous about what is to come.

I know that I wrote little on our trip. I realize this is a bit of a muddle, this diary writing, but I have never before written in a diary and it must take me a little while to become accustomed to the proper form and to decide what is important to include. After all, I cannot write every single detail of every single day. But I will try to write what is important to me and hope that will suffice.

August 28

We are on land at last!

I cannot express my feelings when we disembarked from the small schooner. I wanted to shout and whoop just the way Robbie and James did. Instead I simply stood for a few minutes and tried to get my bearings. I felt a bit odd, as if we were still moving. I decided the best thing would be to walk. And what a joy it was not to be circumscribed by the limits of the ship.

I immediately took a turn around the Fort, which is constructed in an unusual octagonal form. The main building is two storeys high, and the roof is covered with lead. The buildings are made of wood and are surrounded by a stockade. We are on the north bank of the Hayes River and the Fort is built on low ground, surrounded by stagnant water, which lets off a rather unpleasant odour. Under normal circumstances I suppose I would have found the walk unpleasant, but I was delighted to be free!

August 29

These rooms are cold at night, because even though the days are still very warm the rain seems to trap the damp. Passageways that are narrow, and even colder, connect the rooms to each other. Our room has a grate made for burning coal. The bars have been removed so wood can be burned instead. Yet it seems to be constructed in a way that assures the heat will go straight up the chimney. The only warmth one can get is if one stands directly in front of the flames. The roof has been leaking terribly ever since it started to rain.

Still, there is one discovery I have made that endears this place to me despite the lack of any cosiness — there is a library here! I have found a copy of all the plays of Molière and all the plays of Shakespeare. I hope I have time in between my work to do a little reading. What an unexpected treat.

There is a hectic hustle and bustle everywhere, as the Hudson's Bay Company employees stack the animal pelts so they can be loaded onto the schooner, which will take them to the *Prince of Wales* for its return voyage. We settlers have to try to keep out of their way. Robbie is particularly bad at that and I often hear the workers bellowing at him to make way. I try to keep him near me, but I am too busy myself. I must repack all our belongings for the next stage of our journey, so I am washing and mending as quickly as I can.

Father says we are to go on big flat-bottomed boats called York boats, and are to travel south on the Hayes River, and then down the length of a very large lake called Lake Winnipeg. The Forks, where we will settle, is just beyond Lake Winnipeg, at the fork of the Red and Assiniboine rivers — hence the name. What astonishes me is that Father tells me our journey could take two months or more! I had no idea how vast this land was and the distances we would have to traverse.

For this long journey I must pack our belongings in waterproof bags. Apparently there are places where we must get out of the boats and walk. We will be taken by men called Métis, and still others called Cree Indians. The Métis are descendants of French and Indian. They dress in deerskins and wear bright red sashes around their waists. There are even some men who are descendants of Scots and Indians. They are called country born. How strange that a Scotsman would marry a savage.

Later tonight we are to celebrate the end result

of those romances I wrote of earlier. There will be three weddings before we leave.

August 31

I sit in front of the fire as everyone sleeps (still here at York Factory) in order to impart this most terrible news. This evening Father came into the room with a grim look on his face. He sat down on the thin bed and told me to stop my sewing. James strode in behind him, and even Robbie looked up from the small wooden boat he was playing with, sensing that something was wrong.

"Children," Father said, "I have heard some very bad news. I myself am not sure exactly why this has happened, but it has. The settlement at The Forks has been destroyed."

I gasped and asked him how this could possibly be.

"It is this feud between the Hudson's Bay Company and the North West Company," Father replied. "Remember even before we left Scotland, the Nor'Westers tried to discourage us from coming here? As best as I can tell, they see us settlers as a direct threat to their company. They do not want a settlement right in the middle of where they hunt for buffalo. They worry we will drive the buffalo away. They need the pemmican they make from the buffalo to feed their brigades, which go deep into the interior of the land. Because of this," and here Father sighed and shook his head, "the Nor'Westers convinced most of the settlers already at The Forks to leave. They made them offers of land in Upper Canada and paid for their travel. After the settlers left, the Nor'Westers burnt down everything that had been built there, and even drove off the animals."

This is surely a disaster. All we have given up, only to find our destination in ruins?

Father put his head in his hands. "What have I done?" he asked. "Your mother gone, and we headed to such an uncertain future."

"Ach, Father," James said, throwing back his shoulders, "is that the attitude of a Highlander? Will we give up so easily?"

"Mother would never be so quickly defeated," I said, putting on a brave face in an attempt to follow James's example. I steadied my voice. "And nor shall we be, Father."

"Don't worry, Father," Robbie chirped. "I shall learn to shoot with a bow and arrow. I will make us rich in no time!"

Even that did not make Father smile. So you see, dear diary, that we go forward to an uncertain future. But Mother brought us all up to be unafraid, and even though a little part of me trembles, I must pay no mind.

I forgot to mention that the leader of our own party of settlers, Governor Semple, has travelled with us to York Factory. He seems a cultured man, and Mother had told me that she had often read articles written by him in the *Edinburgh Times*. Of course, I saw him rarely on the ship, as he ate at the captain's table, while we would be eating porridge in the hold. I hope he will be able to make peace with these North West Company men, because we still head for The Forks as planned, despite the troubles there.

September 1

Around twenty Indian men all dressed in their finest buckskins arrived at the Post this morning. Father told us that a fur trading ceremony was about to occur. I was thrilled to be able to observe this event.

First the Indians were offered bear steaks, some liquor and some small trinkets. Everyone sat down to eat together. Although we settlers are so many, we were all included in the festivities. The food was delicious.

The Indians produced some beautiful skins, which they gave to the Chief Factor. I was wondering when the trading would begin, or was the trading just everybody giving everyone else gifts?

At that point the Indians and the Hudson's Bay men sat in a circle, and a beautiful long pipe was lit by the man who looked to be the Indian chief. He wore a magnificent headdress of brightly coloured feathers. This pipe was passed around and they each took a puff. Then the actual trading began. A few Indians at a time went into a small room at the back of the Post. Father, who had questioned one of the Hudson's Bay men, explained to me what was happening.

"Now they will trade skins for different goods," he said. "For instance, one beaver skin, if it is of good quality, could be exchanged for twelve needles. Or one beaver skin again could be exchanged for two hatchets or an unruffled shirt, or one pair of shoes, or one plain blanket. A striped blanket would cost more. Now, to get a gun an Indian would need to produce at least twelve good quality beaver skins. Apparently the most plentiful furs are beaver, marten and muskrat. But they also trade in black bear, fox, wolf and more." I found it so interesting and pictured the wealthy people of England walking around in the very furs being traded today. This has been a welcome diversion as we wait for our guides to ready the boats.

September 3

Wish me luck, dear diary, on the next part of the voyage. I cannot say I like the look of those York boats — they seem very open to all the elements. And as it is now the end of summer, some days it is already cold. We are warned that it will become much worse. I worry about Robbie, who is small and has never had a strong constitution, unlike James and me. I intend to ask Father if we couldn't dress Robbie in the animal skins we see the Indians wear. I think he would be far warmer.

But now I really must take my leave. I have more socks to mend and I must do the final packing. Father says we may leave as early as tomorrow morning!

September 6

Dear Diary,

After two days of travel, the first thing I must write about are the bugs. Such a profusion of dreadful creatures could not be imagined, and

yet they exist! Our first day on the boats introduced us to almost all of these horrid things.
There are small black flies, which find any little
piece of skin that is not covered, and bite, causing
a sharp pain. Then there are the mosquitoes that
seem to arrive in huge clouds, especially in the
shady areas as we paddle beneath the trees, and
at dusk before we land for the night. These
bloodsucking monsters leave huge welts behind
them. Robbie in particular is suffering terribly
from mosquito bites, each of which is swelling to
the size of a coin. Mine have not swollen as badly,
but the old ones seem to itch as violently as the
new ones, until I feel like one huge itch.
Sometimes, when no one can see me, I cry from
sheer misery. But this is not the end of it. No,
there are the big horseflies that buzz around our
heads, and if they can gain purchase either on
our heads or anywhere on our bodies, will bite.
There are the yellow jackets and big wasps, and
always the danger of tipping over one of their
nests and disturbing them. This happened to
James on our first day out. He was chased all the
way to the river that evening after we had
camped, and his only escape was to dive beneath
the icy water. He has come down with a dreadful
cold and chills.

September 7

One of the Indians motioned me over as I was bathing James's brow with cool water this evening after we camped. I was nervous, as I know the Indians are savages, but I noticed Kate smirking at me so I held my head up and walked over to where the Indian stood, knife in hand! Was he going to slit my throat in front of everyone? Father was off hunting in the woods, as were most of the men. I was quite defenceless. He raised his knife and a cold chill ran down my spine. He put the knife against a willow tree and peeled some bark off, then handed it to me. He walked over to the kettle and pointed to the water, as if I should throw it in, which I did. And then he raised an imaginary glass as if he were drinking, and pointed to James. I understood it would make a tea. And when James drank it his fever dropped in almost no time! At home, Mother, you would take a thin rind of an orange, roll it inside out and place it inside the nostril of whichever one of us was ill, but here we have no oranges. I hope you feel I did the right thing.

The same Indian then showed me how to rub mud on our skin to ease the pain of the bites and to prevent new ones. (This gave Robbie relief almost immediately and I am very grateful.) He is a tall man whose name, according to one of our Métis guides who speaks English, is Running Fox, and he looks a bit like his name, having a sharp nose and a thin face, and he moves quickly as he goes about his duties. He has a severe look about him, but when I hesitantly went over to him and said, "Thank you," he smiled — showing very sharp teeth!

September 8

It is not easy to take the time to write. We are up every morning by 7. We make camp at around 4 if the day has been particularly hard, or as late as 6 or 7 if we must keep going before we can find a place to camp. The light is gone by the time camp is set up and it is not easy to write by the fire, although I will attempt it if I cannot ever write in daylight. Today the hunters shot seven geese and I can smell them cooking as I write. I am famished.

I am quite in awe of the men rowing these boats. They go for hours at a time without a break, in a feat of endurance I would not have credited had I not seen it with my own eyes.

September 9

We are still on the Hayes River. It rises, apparently, from here on, so we are going upstream, and today was our first taste of what that means. There is a series of small falls and rapids, and since we are going against the current it has become too hard to row. Our guides and the strongest of the settlers, which, of course, includes James and Father, tied ropes to the boats and had to pull them along the shore. The rest of us walked. The terrain is quite flat. Father says it is called tundra, but we are warned that it will soon become more rugged and more difficult to traverse.

We are twenty to a boat, and Kate somehow ended up in our boat. She is travelling with her father, her mother long dead. She has a brother already in the New World, although she says little about him. Now that we are walking the girl never leaves my side. She is like the pesky bugs, hovering about me constantly!

September 10

This morning I slipped on a rock and Kate, who is always nearby, grabbed me. I was forced to thank her, and she smiled in that annoying way she has and said, "Well, you are lucky I was there. Good posture is no help on this trip, is it?" I think she did it just so she could lord it over me and continue with her ceaseless teasing.

September 15

The boats were emptied of their cargo today and the women and children were told to carry as much as we could. We are beginning what is called a *portage* where the boats are moved by land, as there is no possibility to row them any farther in the water. The guides tie a thick band over their foreheads, and the larger bundles are attached to this band. The packs, or pieces as they call them, are massive and heavy and I marvel at the strength needed to carry them. The boats are then placed on log rollers and pulled by rope. This is a long and difficult process and the men appear to hate it. As happy as they were to row these huge boats, they are unhappy during this stage of the trip.

And they are not the only ones. We must carry heavy loads up and over huge craggy rocks. Father and the other elders had no idea this trip would be so difficult, and I hear quite a lot of complaining at night around the campfire.

There is one bright spot. As the weather cools off, especially at night, the mosquitoes at least are diminishing.

September 17

Kate never misses an opportunity to make me miserable. Father tells me to ignore her and will not let me retaliate. And I know, Mother dear, that you would not allow me to utter a mean word no matter what the provocation. I try very hard not to respond to her. But last night I was unable to quell my anger.

I am not a squeamish person, but one thing I cannot abide, and that is a snake. I made the mistake of shrieking when one crossed my path as we were walking. Kate, as she always does, was walking just behind me. She immediately recognized my fear, and last night I was woken from a deep sleep by a snake slithering over my face. I leapt up screaming and woke the entire campsite. I saw her laughing and knew she had been the cause of my humiliation. I took a step toward her and almost slapped her, only stopping when James caught my wrist.

All day today the Indians made signs with their hands as if they were snakes, and grinned when they saw me. The younger boys teased me mercilessly. What a devil that Kate is.

September 25

The Métis speak French and the Cree speak their own language, so it is often confusing to try to follow their orders. But we try.

Little Justin Mackenzie broke his leg today when he slipped on wet moss and leaves. The men used a tree branch to set it, but then Justin's older brother Evan had to pull him on a makeshift stretcher.

September 27

I should describe a little about our camp.

When we reach our final destination of the day we are given tents to set up. We cover the ground where we sleep with an oilskin and over that we place a deerskin. This combination keeps us dry and there are many blankets to keep us warm. We cook over an open fire. I mix flour, water and a little lard to make fresh bannock. The boatmen put pemmican in a pot, with some water and whatever roots they can find. They call this rubaboo. It has an odd taste, sometimes bitter depending on the roots, but Father assured me that it is nourishing. He makes sure we eat every drop of the stew we are offered — even Robbie, who swore he would never touch the stuff the first time he smelled it. The pemmican itself is made from dried buffalo meat, fat and berries. It is easy to pack and lasts forever and is very important to the fur traders, as it is their staple diet.

It was this pemmican that sparked all the trouble at The Forks. As we've been travelling we have heard more news as everyone shares what they know when we sit around the campfire. The Governor of Lord Selkirk's earlier settlement, Miles Macdonell, proclaimed that no pemmican could be removed from the Red River Settlement. He feared his settlers would starve without enough pemmican. This angered the North West Company, who assumed this was all a ploy by the Hudson's Bay Company to put them out of business — as Father told us earlier, they travel far to the west and north, and cannot do so without pemmican. And they fear that our settlement might drive off the buffalo altogether. Naturally, every night the talk turns to what our reception will be and whether we will be safe.

As for me I think about the buffalo. I cannot

wait to see these beasts. They sound like something out of mythology.

October 1

It has been nothing but *portages* and walking, crying children, and men and women with sore feet and backs. But soon we will reach a place called Oxford House and today we were back in the boats, crossing Holy Lake. It seemed like a gift from God as we sat and rested, instead of tramping over the dangerous ground. The sun shone and as we sat in the boat it seemed we had arrived in Paradise. The landscape has changed greatly. Shrubs and pines give way to majestic old trees: oak, elm, poplar and maple. The leaves are bright yellow with an occasional dash of red, and today I look through them into the deep blue sky, a colour blue I have never before seen, and I feel we are blessed by God.

October 2

We have reached Oxford House. It is another Hudson's Bay Post. We are still in tents, as there is no room for all of us in the buildings, but tonight we are eating fresh fish, and tomorrow we can wash our clothes!

October 3

Clean clothes. Heaven. I spent the day mending and washing.

October 10

Ever since we left the comfort of Oxford House days ago, the wind has blown cold in our faces, the rain fell, the boats struggled to stay upright and we did not know if each moment would be our last. My only consolation as I prayed for the safety of my family was that if we were to die, I would see you, Mother, all that much sooner. It is getting too cold at night to write and has been too wet.

October 12

We have arrived at Jack River Post. Some of our company have relatives here who came out to meet us. A young fellow, Jim Dickson, had baked a maple sugar cake to present to his parents. He said it showed proof of the goodness of the country.

October 13

We had a wonderful party last night where we ate and danced reels and jigs. What a relief to be able to rest. But we must leave tomorrow, to begin our journey south, down Lake Winnipeg. It could take us weeks, they say.

I do not expect to write again until we reach The Forks. It has become very cold at night.

October 15

It has become so cold my hand cannot hold my pen.

November 3

We arrived today at The Forks!

We are ensconced in the main building at Fort Douglas, in a small room. I sit by the fire and on the rough wooden table is a cruisie lamp which gives me just enough light to see these pages.

So much has happened since my last entry, and weeks have passed. Near the end of the journey we had to endure another trial. We ran out of food. The hunters were only finding small game, not nearly enough to feed such a large group. The pemmican was gone. We became weaker by the day as we subsisted on a watery stew of roots, some sort of wild turnip. Robbie became pale, and he shivered easily as he had no food inside him to keep him warm. (And dear diary, so did I, although I never would have complained and worried Father.) It seemed after a while that we would be travelling forever and never reach our destination.

Being on Lake Winnipeg was once again like being on the sea, it is so large. Our boats had to hug the shore because the winds would have been too much for us out in the open. At times all I could think of was my empty stomach, and I'm afraid I barely noticed my surroundings. Finally, we had the good fortune to run into the boat party of Governor Semple, who had gone on ahead of us. We were told that we would be at The Forks within days. And when he saw the pitiful state we were in he opened his own personal rations of cheese and biscuits to us, which were enough to see us through the last couple of days as our boats travelled down what is called the Red River out of Lake Winnipeg. Winnipeg means muddy water, and the Red River certainly has a muddy look.

This morning when we arrived at The Forks the sun shone and Jasper McKay played his bagpipes. On the rough wooden dock, waiting for us, were thirteen families — the only settlers who had not been driven away by the North West Company. Many in our party had relatives on that dock. In fact, the reason they had come to the New World was because of the urging of relatives who had come before. We leapt onto the dock as our boats pulled in. Everyone seemed to talk at once. We had no relatives there, but Father knew some of those who came from the Highlands.

It was chaos as news was exchanged. Tears flowed, people called to one another. I looked around anxiously to get a good view of our new home, but it all looked similar to the landscape we had just travelled, trees, bushes and shrubs near the river, tall grass and shrub farther on. I could not really see beyond this so I was anxious to go exploring. I was about to suggest this to James and Robbie when Father hurried over to us and stated, "We cannot even unpack."

"But why not, Father?" I asked, dreading what he was to say.

"Because the settlers have not had a chance to rebuild since the attack. Nothing is ready for us. Apparently there is not enough food for us to spend the winter here. It appears that we will have to leave The Forks almost immediately, before it gets too cold for us to travel. We are to go south to a place called Pembina. It is about a 60-mile trip. Miles Macdonell has built a fort there, Fort Daer, just for the settlers. The buffalo roam near there in the winter and we must follow them if we are to have enough to eat over the winter." He shook his head. "This group had to go all the way back north to Jack River. They returned in August and began to rebuild what the Nor'Westers burned, but winter has overtaken both them and us."

I cannot yet believe it even though I am reporting it in these pages. Such a long and difficult trip, only to discover home is still beyond our grasp. It is heartbreaking news that we must spend an entire winter away, and that it will only be in the spring that we can return, to begin our new lives here at The Forks.

November 4

Dear Diary,

I have stolen a few moments to write. The party could not ready itself in time to leave today, so we leave tomorrow at first light. Our first night spent here at The Forks, or Colony Gardens as the first group of settlers call it, was happy enough. After writing to you, dear diary, I joined the festivities in the Fort's big room. Bagpipes were played and people danced. The settlers here dance what is called a Red River jig. It is a mix of a Scottish reel and a Cree dance. George Dunn played the fiddle. A man and a woman face each other, balancing up on their toes. They dance back and forth, feet flying in fancy steps I could hardly note, they move so quickly, until one grows tired and another takes either his or her place.

The men drank far too much and James was quite sick later on that evening. Even Father seemed to be coming out of his shell a little and he danced with Robbie, making him very happy.

I met Alice Connor, who is thirteen — only a year older than me — and was very friendly toward me. She pointed out that there were some very good-looking young men in our party, especially my own brother James.

"How old is he?" she asked me.

"Fifteen," I answered.

She nodded as if she had made her mind up that he would be for her. And somehow she managed to get him to dance with her. I noticed that Kate would not dance. I suspected it was because she has no natural grace. But I had no time to worry about Kate. The night was a night to enjoy. We ate partridges that had been cooked in a pit, making them tender and juicy. There was fresh bread because some of the grain had been salvaged from the vicious attacks; there was wild rice, which has an almost nutty flavour. It was heaven just to fill our stomachs, and the fact that it was so delicious was an added treat. This morning we were given maple syrup on top of fried bread. It is sap from the maple tree and is quite wonderful.

The thermometer at the Fort said it was ten degrees below zero when we arose. I knew that the clothes we had with us would not protect us sufficiently on this trip to Pembina. I was especially concerned about Robbie. There was such a hustle and bustle it was almost impossible to find anyone, but I managed to locate Running Fox, who had helped me before. I pointed to his clothes and then to Robbie, and shivered as if Robbie were cold. Running Fox nodded and pointed to the silk kerchief I often wore around my neck. I understood right away that he wanted it. Mother, you had bought it for me last year when I turned twelve. I treasured it more than anything — anything except Robbie's health. So I gave it to Running Fox and he returned with trousers made from deerskin, which fitted Robbie perfectly. He also gave me a small blanket to tie about Robbie's shoulders with a piece of sinew. I thanked him and he smiled that foxy smile of his.

It was then I heard the most dreadful noise: a horrible screeching, which made my teeth hurt. I turned toward the sound and saw the strangest sight. A large cart, taller than myself, was moving slowly toward me, pulled by a horse. Behind it came others, some pulled by the men of the colony, some by oxen. The carts have huge wheels, which are made entirely of wood. They were laden with goods.

James came up behind me. "Two of our trunks are going on those carts," he said. "Aren't they strange? They're called Red River carts. See how the whole thing is held together by strips of buffalo hide and wooden pegs? That's because they had to invent a way to build them without using nails. Nails are so hard to find here that when the York boats finish their trips they burn them entirely just to retrieve the nails."

"What have you got there?" I said to James, looking down at something he was holding behind his back.

"Aah," he smiled. "I traded for this." And with a flourish he brought out a bow and arrow. "Robbie wants one too, and I think he should have one before long. You and Father baby him far too much."

Robbie is ten years old now, that is true. I

believe I was remiss and did not even mention his birthday in September. It must have been one of those days when I was unable to write. "He isn't strong, though," I objected.

"He will need to be strong," James insisted. "It will be good for him to get out and hunt."

I sighed and bit my lip, and tried to think what you would do, Mother. Perhaps James is right and Robbie needs to become stronger.

"Look," James said, pointing at his feet. "I also traded for these." He was wearing a pair of moccasins like the Indians'. "They are much easier to walk in and they are warmer than our boots."

I looked down at my worn boots, one of which already has a hole in the sole. "I wish I could have a pair, and Robbie and Father too," I added.

"Do you have anything you can trade for them?" James asked.

"I already traded Mother's scarf for warm trousers and a blanket for Robbie," I said. "I do have the necklace you made me last year."

James could see my distress. I hated to part with it. He had crafted me a necklace of smooth stones, a thing of beauty. James is very talented and can make rings, bracelets and necklaces.

"Don't worry, Isobel," he said. "In the spring I shall collect the most beautiful stones from the riverbed here, and make you an even nicer necklace for your thirteenth birthday. I promise."

The necklace was in a small bag of belongings that had not yet been put back on the York boat or the cart. I found it and looked around for someone to trade with. I could not find Running Fox, but I noticed a young Indian girl about my age. Perhaps she would like a necklace even better than Running Fox would. She wore a buckskin dress with beautiful beads sewn onto the front, a wide sash, and moccasins that reached all the way up her legs. I ran over to her and got her attention by saying hello, which she seemed to understand. I pointed to her moccasins and then counted on my fingers to the number 3, and then showed her the necklace. Her eyes lit up when she saw the necklace, shining red and purple. She nodded and motioned for me to wait. She returned not with moccasins, but with skins and sinew, which obviously was to be used for thread. Then she motioned as if she were walking and then as if she were sewing and then as if she were sleeping. I think she meant that she would also be walking with us, and that she would show me how to sew the moccasins at night. She had a nice face, round with black eyes and a big smile. For a moment I forgot that she was a savage, for she

seemed a girl just like myself. I held out the necklace for her. She took it and gave me the skins
and the sinew. I smiled and said thank you, and
she mimicked my words and said thank you, but
with such a funny accent I had to laugh. She
looked sad then, as if I had hurt her feelings. I
reminded myself that the savages are probably
like children and must be treated kindly. I put a
solemn look on my face and said thank you again
and she said thank you again, too, her happy
smile returning.

I ran to find James. He thought I had done
very well and I promised that by the morning the
whole family would have moccasins.

"Mother could not have done better," he said
to me.

Tears came to my eyes. I know what he said is
not true, Mother, but I am trying to take your
place as best I can.

November 14

I write now for the first time since we left The
Forks. It has been a dreadful journey, ten brutish
days — but I get ahead of myself. It may take me
a few days of writing to tell everything that happened. But at least now I sit by a fire and my

hands are warm enough to hold my pen.

We were finally ready to go on the morning of our second day, the thirteen families that had remained, and our entire group. We would be split into two groups, those walking behind the Red River carts, which were filled with goods, and those in the boats. A Métis or Indian was in each boat as a guide. All the young children were placed in the boats since they could not possibly walk so far. Robbie was among them, but I was deemed too old and so I was forced to part with him, which made me very anxious, until at the last minute I managed to squeeze onto the boat beside him. I know James says I baby him, but someone has to watch over him and Father was unable to go in that boat, as parents who had *very* small children naturally had to accompany them. Much to my dismay I quickly noted that Kate was also in our boat. I turned to her and said, "Why are you not walking? You are certainly strong enough."

Kate replied, "Listen to Miss High and Mighty! Why are you not walking?"

"I have little Robbie to care for," I informed her.

"And I have myself to care for," she retorted.

"And where would your father be?" I asked. "Would he not want you to be with him?"

Kate looked down quickly and it was the first time I had ever noticed that she seemed unsure of herself. "My father . . . my father . . . looks after himself." She raised her eyes defiantly. "And I look after myself."

I was shocked by her reply. I thought back to what I knew of her father and could remember little. He seemed a quiet man, if dour, who never caused any trouble the way his daughter did. But when I thought about it I realized that I had never seen him discipline Kate over her behaviour; in fact, I rarely remembered seeing them together.

Robbie pulled my attention away from her at that moment. "How do I look?" he crowed, showing off his new trousers. "As fine as the Indians?"

"You look to me to be the finest young man in the New World," I said, giving him a hug and kiss.

I was glad he had his blanket pinned about him, as a cold north wind was blowing harder by the minute. The temperature, rather than rising as it should be, seemed to be dropping. Clouds scurried across a pale blue sky.

The men rowed hard all day with only a brief halt for lunch. That night we stopped, but had to make camp without Father and James, who were with the other group and probably well back of us. In order to cheer up the older children, some of whom were without their parents, I led them in song around the campfire. We sang "The Bonnie Banks of Loch Lomand."

Later

This is a long story. But I want to record it here. I can imagine myself reading this to Robbie's children one day, and them laughing at their dear dad. So I continue:

When we awoke the next morning it was to a terrible sight. The river had frozen during the night and the boats could go no farther. We would have to walk. And me with a hole in my boot. Most of the boxes and trunks had to be left behind, as the fathers who had been rowing found themselves carrying their children instead. Robbie and I were the fortunate ones, our belongings being on the Red River carts travelling behind us with those on foot. Snow began to fall. It whipped into our faces. I regretted terribly that the Indian girl who had promised to help me make moccasins was walking behind us with the other group. I had the skins in my bag, but in the meantime my boots hurt and I could feel the cold coming through the hole. Robbie's boots had no holes but they were worn and not as easy to walk in as moccasins would be. My cheeks began to feel almost numb. My skirts dragged, often catching on bushes or brambles. When we finally stopped for the night I was chilled through even though I had wrapped my shawl as tightly around me as I could. It was no match for the fierce wind. I understood why the deerskin would be so warm — it would keep out the wind.

We made hot tea by the fire, and our guides cooked some rabbit and birds, which they had managed to shoot with bow and arrow. We settled down for the night in our tents and woke the next morning to find the ground covered in snow. There was no trail or path, so we followed the guides, trudging through the snow. I kept a tight hand on Robbie all the time, afraid that he would wander off and freeze.

That night we snuggled together under blankets in the tent, along with Kate (whose devious pranks seemed to diminish the more it snowed and the colder she got) and a number of other children. I'm not sure what it was, but something woke me in the middle of the night. It was pitch black and I could see nothing and yet I knew right away that Robbie was not there.

"Robbie . . . Robbie," I hissed. But there was no

reply. I shook Kate awake. "Have you seen Robbie?

"No," she grunted. "I'm sleeping."

I pulled my shawl tightly around me and ran out into the night. The campfire was burning low in the centre of the tents, but I could not see Robbie in its light.

I ran to find some of the men who had been rowing the boats. "My brother Robbie is gone, he's gone from the tent!" I cried.

"He probably just needed to relieve himself, lass," one of the men said kindly. "You mustn't worry. He's sure to turn up any second."

Of course, I thought, that must be it. Perhaps I should have tied a cord between us so that he couldn't wander off by himself. But he's ten, I reminded myself, not a child. He shall be fine.

I felt like crying, but I remembered that Mother was not there and Father was not there and James was not there and that I was in charge of Robbie and that I had to calm myself and try to find him. It is true, I thought, he probably did simply go out to relieve himself and perhaps he would be back quickly. But then I couldn't help but consider that perhaps he had got lost in the white snow and couldn't find his way back. The moon was behind the clouds, and away from the fire he would be unable to see a finger in front of his face.

And then, dear diary, dear Mother, I got one of my feelings. Many times, Mother, you told me of your mother and her sixth sense. Sometimes you used to say that you thought I had inherited it, and other times you would say no, I had not, because I showed the signs so rarely. But every once in a while I would get a *feeling*, and you had taught me to always listen to my feeling and to trust it.

I had a feeling that Robbie would have gone behind a tent so as not to get lost, but once there the light from the fire would be blocked. It would be easy to get lost then. I told the men that perhaps he had done that and so we hurried back to my tent, the men holding up burning logs from the fire so we could see.

We were encamped in a small clearing surrounded by trees. Some of the bushes seemed to have less snow on them than others, perhaps after Robbie had rustled them, but we could not see his footprints. We slogged our way through the snow. And then, in the silence of the night, because the snow makes everything so quiet, I heard him crying.

"Robbie!" I shouted.

"Isobel," he called back.

We followed his voice until Robbie was in my arms. He was shivering with cold. One of the men picked him up and carried him back to the camp-site. I covered him up with blankets as soon as he was inside the tent.

"I feel so foolish," he whispered to me.

"Never mind, little one," I soothed him. "You didn't know how to find your way. Now you go right to sleep. We have a long day tomorrow."

November 15

I continue my story now. I could write no more last night, still feeling exhausted and weak.

The day after Robbie's near disaster, the sun shone bright and the snow glittered and sparkled with such glory it seemed we had woken to a magical land. But with the sun, the temperature took a ferocious dip and we found ourselves to be woefully inadequately dressed. I kept a tight hold on Robbie. I would not let him out of my sight.

A young lad, name of Peter, had befriended him, and walked along with us. He was from one of the thirteen families that had stayed. He was certainly not shy! He told us a little of their story as we walked.

"We came on the ship *Prince of Wales*," he said in the funny little high voice he has. "The voyage was very rough. Was your voyage rough?" he asked, but he didn't wait for an answer. "Our voyage was very, very rough and then the fever struck. Typhus, it was. I was probably one of the only people who didn't get it; seems like everyone got sick. My mother almost died from it and my little sister too, but we were lucky, we were the lucky ones. My Auntie Mary she did succumb and was thrown off the ship into the cruel waters of the ocean."

Robbie gasped. "My mother died too, but she was buried in the ground. I would not like to see her thrown to the fish."

"Three or four died and were thrown off the ship," Peter continued. "It was a terrible sight. When we landed in Churchill the captain was so frightened of the illness and so anxious to get us off the ship that he would not take us to York Factory. So we were stranded on the barren rocks with nothing — no food, no shelter."

I stopped him for a moment. "He simply deserted you there?" I asked. "Why, he should be thrown in irons!"

"That's what I think," Peter agreed.

Kate had come up alongside us and was now

tagging along. "Ach," she said, "listen to that boy whining."

"He is simply telling us what happened," I objected. "You cannot accuse him of whining — not with the difficult journey they had."

Peter went on to tell us that they had had to winter where they'd been left, and then in the spring had to walk all the way to York Factory. Finally in June of last year they arrived at The Forks, where they built Fort Douglas. They wintered there, but that was when a fellow called Duncan Cameron of the North West Company convinced many of the settlers to leave for Upper Canada. It was not only his honeyed words that worked on the settlers though. At the same time the settlers' crops were burned, as were their buildings, and the people were threatened. And yet Peter's family were simply too stubborn to leave with the rest. I certainly admired them.

I was also glad to see Robbie making a friend. They continued to talk as we walked and I'm sure it made the time go quicker and took their minds off the dreadful cold.

Each day blended into the next as we trudged through the snow. One day it warmed up, which at first we believed to be a welcome relief, until the snow turned to ice and it became dangerous to set one foot in front of the other. Then the snow came again. I noticed that Robbie's face was becoming red and sore. It seemed that he and probably the rest of us were suffering from some kind of a snow-burn, which must be similar to sunburn.

There was little food and the children were depleted from the long, cold, dreary walk, but finally we arrived here at Pembina and the fort, Fort Daer. It is just a group of huts, nothing more, but it looked like heaven to us. The other families were not yet here, so we settled into various huts, where we immediately made fires and then hot tea. The huts are no more than one-room affairs, but at least we are protected from the elements.

The men made rubaboo for the entire company. I cooked bannock and tried to get the small children settled under big buffalo robes and blankets. And that brings us up to the present moment, waiting for our families to join us.

November 16

Father and James were so happy to see Robbie and me. Father immediately tried to find us a place of our own, but there are too few huts. Some of our party were already staying in storage sheds. So Father and the other men have to build enough huts for everyone, and even then we will have to share. Today they cut down trees.

November 17

The huts were built today, using round unfinished wood and filling in the cracks with clay. The floors are bare earth. The men have time to do no more.

Somehow Kate and her father have ended up with us. And it is from our new little hut, dear diary, that I write to you now. If Kate dislikes me so, why is she always hovering about me? I tried to tell Father that we would be better off with another family, but he would hear none of it, saying that we were lucky to share with only two instead of a family of five.

November 19

The snow has melted again and the Indians near us are going on a buffalo hunt. Father says they are Cree and that the band we met at The Forks is called the Saulteaux, although there were Cree there, too, as well as Ojibwa. They are all, according to the settlers who have been here longer, very friendly and helpful to us.

What excitement! I assumed that I would see none of the hunt, but in fact I will be able to witness almost all of it. The Indians have their camp very near to our small fort and it is here that they made what is called a pound. The shaman, who is their medicine man and their spiritual leader — rather like our elder, I suppose — chose the site. Everyone, settlers and Indians alike, followed him as he performed this task. He stopped at a thicket 30 to 40 feet in diameter. As soon as he indicated that this would be the spot, I watched in fascination as the young men of the band proceeded to clear it. They cut the brush and the trees and then heaped it all up to make a wall about 10 to 15 feet high. Two tall trees were left at the entrance and a log was secured between them at the same height as the wall. This took almost the entire day, and almost all of the young men in our party joined in to help, in the hope that the Indians would share the hunt with us. I had to almost sit on Robbie, as he is too young to be wielding such sharp blades, but he managed to scramble away from me and helped the other young Indian boys drag the bushes once they had been cut.

November 20

Today something called a chute was built. The young men cut down more trees and bushes. These they lashed together and made bundles, which were stacked about 30 yards apart from each other and about 4 feet high. This chute was at least a mile long, or so James told me — he helped build the entire structure. Just in front of the enclosure the chute takes a sharp turn so that the buffalo, as they run, cannot see that they are headed for a dead end. It seems to me that they must be very clever animals or they would not notice such things.

As night fell the shaman conducted a ceremony in his tent. I could hear him singing, but I don't know what the ceremony consisted of — praying for a hunt, I suppose. But if they do not pray to our God, to whom do these savages pray? I shall endeavour to find this out.

November 21

James tells me that the buffalo will be here soon and that we will be able to watch as they are killed in the pound. Apparently the young men have ridden off to find the herd. They will slap the ground with their robes, which makes a loud noise. This frightens the buffalo into motion. James says that the young Indians on horseback control them. If the herd goes off course, the hunters will veer their horses at them. The buffalo then veer toward the hunters in order to cut the hunters off. The hunters — knowing they will do this — use this tactic to make sure the buffalo go in the right direction. Again, I think that they must be rather clever creatures — our Highland sheep would run in the other direction if a horse came after them! Once the buffalo are in the chute the hunters make large motions to scare them into moving forward. And once they are in the pound, they are killed.

November 22

Now that Kate is living in the same hut as us, it is my responsibility to make sure that she does her share of household chores. Water must be lugged from the river. Clothes desperately need washing and mending after so long a journey; and, of course, we must cook.

My new friend Alice gave me my first cooking lesson suited to this new land. The men had managed to kill some deer. I went to her hut to watch her make haggis.

"It's not very different," she said, "from the way we used to make it in the old country, except here we use deer instead of sheep."

Alice, her mother and Alice's older sister Bettie began to prepare the haggis as I looked on. They had the stomach of the deer prepared already. Into it they put the heart and lungs of the deer, the shredded fat from the different organs, oatmeal, and a bowl of blood that they harvested from the carcass. They gave me a knife, and together we shredded all the lean meat. Finally when everything was in and stitched up, the stomach was suspended high above the flames of the open fire. Mrs. Connor then invited our entire family and Kate and her father to eat with them. It was extremely delicious and there was almost a festive atmosphere in the little hut. Alice made sure that James noticed what a good cook she was. Kate seemed so thankful for a decent meal that even she managed to keep quiet for the most part.

I cannot participate in Alice's interest in young men. After all, the only young men here are poor and unlearned. James has three times the learning of any of the other young men, because of our dear mother. No, I shall wait for something better.

I want to sew the moccasins but the Indian girl

must be too busy preparing for the coming hunt, as she waves me off whenever I motion sewing to her.

November 24

It is hard to describe the sights I have just seen. How can I do justice in these pages to the magnificent beasts and to their noble hunters? This is a sight, Mother dear, that would have thrilled you!

At about midday I was mending a shirt of Father's, sitting near the fire for as much light as possible. Kate, under my strict supervision, was mending socks, grumbling incessantly about how boring it was and how she should be out hunting buffalo. Frankly, I should have been quite happy if she chose to do so. Suddenly we heard pounding and thudding and the ground shook beneath our feet. We threw down our work, grabbed our shawls and ran with the rest of the settlers to the place of the pound.

I have never seen a buffalo before, and although I had been told that they were large, I never could have imagined a beast so strong, powerful and dangerous. And yet the young men seemed to have no fear as they directed them into the corral. On horseback they followed the buffalo inside the enclosure, riding directly beside them, arrows ready. They shot the beasts and one by one they fell. I am not sure I took a breath from the beginning until the end, and then I felt quite faint from the excitement.

The shaman sang a song, shaking a rattle at the same time. The women followed directly, slicing open the buffalo. A man, wailing and crying, went to each creature and began to cut up the insides and to give them to different people. Little boys who ran into the enclosure took the intestines and threw them over the branches of the tree that had been left in the centre of the enclosure. As they did this they imitated the crow, making harsh sounds. Then the little girls of the village ran to the shaman's tipi, bringing wood. When this was done the crying man gave each little girl a small piece of heart fat and each little boy a piece of buffalo tongue.

Then the women got to work at a speed that I found astonishing. They skinned the buffalo and hung the skins over tree branches. Then they began to scrape the hides. They motioned for the women settlers who were watching to come and help, and so we did. I was given a small sharp knife that had probably been obtained by trading furs. I had to hold my breath because of the strong stench of blood and guts. I scraped away the flesh as best I could.

"Don't faint, Little Princess," Kate called to me. "Why, you look quite green!" She laughed as she worked away.

I would not let her see me squirm, so I gritted my teeth and worked hard all afternoon. Near evening we finished and the Indian women took the hides and stretched them on the ground, holding them down with stakes.

I shall sleep well tonight. Never have I felt so worn out, not even after our terrible walk.

November 29

I have been so exhausted every evening that I have been remiss about writing in your pages. I think the hardest thing to convey is how strange and different everything is. Although I always dreamed of a better life when we lived in Scotland, everything was safe and familiar. In the morning we would do our chores. The boys would help Father in the fields and I would help Mother, cleaning, mending and, of course, cooking the large meals that the men needed to sustain them as they worked.

I am trying to establish some sort of order in our days here, as I'm sure Mother would have wanted. Father says that I am still a child and that I should go out and play. Play! What can he be thinking? It is up to me to make sure that this hut is clean, that the clothes are mended, that there is food to eat, and that Robbie is properly supervised. And I also must think about Robbie's education. I am sure Mother would want him to continue to study, just as I'm sure she would want me to continue to perfect the things she felt important. At least when I write in these pages it is a chance for me to practise my penmanship and my writing skills. There are no books here outside of the Bible, and this is a great trial for me, and for James, who loves to read. Whenever Father went on one of his rare visits to town in the old country, he bought second-hand books for us, and every night we would take turns reading to one another. I suspect there were very few other families, poor tenant farmers, who behaved in such a way, but Mother never let us forget that she came from the gentry. My favourite books were the poets.

I have begun to read the Bible aloud at night, at least as a way to keep up our tradition. Kate's father is a sullen man who barely speaks a word. He sits quietly as I read, but I do not think he is listening or paying any attention. Kate, surprisingly enough, seems to like to be read to, although she would never admit such a thing.

Father says there might be trouble with provisions for the winter. The weather has turned bitter and I can see he is worried about how we will survive. Without Mother's cheerful optimism and fearlessness it is harder for him not to doubt his decision to bring us all here.

November 30

A strange thing happened first thing this morning. When I took my long flannel nightdress off, tiny bright white lights shot off from it in every direction. I was startled and gasped. Kate, who shares an oilskin with me on the floor, noticed and laughed at my fear, but when I challenged her she could not explain the cause of such a strange phenomenon.

"Perhaps they are little ghosts," I said to her, almost positive it was not true, but unable to resist trying to frighten her. She turned quite pale at that idea, then caught herself out and said, "That is just silly. Ghosts are big and white."

"Maybe not in the New World," I replied, my voice low and menacing.

I have never seen Kate, or any young woman, dress herself so quickly and make for the outdoors — which I assume she felt was safe from the little ghosts. Still, I do wonder what could cause such a strange thing.

December 10

Father says we may have to leave Fort Daer and follow the Indians in order to survive the winter. The Indians are travelling farther south, tracking the buffalo. And they will share their hunt with us if we help the way we did the last time.

This small hut we live in now is cold. The wind blows through the cracks in the logs that are filled in only with clay. But at least it is a shelter. If we go with the Indians where will we live? And even though we still have some of the meat the Indians shared from the hunt, it will not be enough to last us the winter.

Father is disgusted by the Hudson's Bay Company's poor foresight. How did they think we were to survive? There are some mutterings amongst the men that the Company never meant to support us at all, and that they regret giving Lord Selkirk the land. Perhaps they hope to starve us out!

Today I met with the Indian girl who promised to help me sew the moccasins. And finally this afternoon she sat with me and, in exchange for a real needle instead of the bone she normally uses, she taught me how to make moccasins. I used the skins I traded for, and now have moccasins for the entire family.

She is called White Loon, which I think is a beautiful name.

December 12

White Loon has taught me a few Cree words and I have taught her a few English words. I think she is older than I believed her to be at first, perhaps twenty. Her face is so smooth and pretty that she seems no more than my age, but I now realize she is a developed woman. She has a calm and cheerful personality. I am surprised because, as a savage, I expected her to be coarse and barbaric in her manners.

December 15

Alice tells me that the Indians have been very kind to the settlers since they have been here. She has begun to spend time with me and White Loon, trying to learn a little of their language as well. Kate stays well away and makes endless comments when we are back in our hut, about fraternizing with savages. Secretly I wonder if she is not right. Perhaps it is not good company to keep. Perhaps one day White Loon will harm me in some way if I say or do something that insults her.

December 17

It will soon be New Year's. We will be lucky to have any kind of meal. And what can I give my family as presents for Handsel Monday?

December 18

My entries into your pages have been shorter and shorter. That is because it is so horribly cold I can barely hold my pen. We shall be packing what we can soon — only our warmest clothes. And we shall be following the Indians. Dear diary, I do not know how much I will be able to write.

It appears that all of the settlers who go will be working as some sort of serf or slave to the Indians in order to share in their hunt and to be fed. Father believes it is a humiliation we should not have to suffer, but he also believes it would be foolish to stand on pride and starve to death here in Pembina. Did I mention that Pembina is the name the Indians call the berries that they add to the pemmican to flavour it?

I suspect the tents will be dark at night and during the day it will be difficult to write outdoors without my hand dropping off. With no gloves I believe skin could actually freeze.

December 27

Father has returned to his former state of grief, approaching his first New Year's without Mother. I, too, feel bereft. James was gone all day, hunting. Robbie picked a fight with Peter. I think it was because he was angry but unable to think why. I cannot bear to contemplate all the wonderful holidays we had together and then to compare it with our situation now.

I made mittens for Robbie from a rabbit James managed to shoot with his bow and arrow. James and I made the foot into a talisman and put it on a cord for Father. And for James I have mended every one of his shirts. I would have done it anyway, but I will give it to him as a gift, as I have nothing better I can give him.

January 2, 1816

Hogmanay turned out much better than I would have imagined. Father gave me ink he had bought at the Fort. James made me a beautiful little necklace that he whittled from wood and tied on a piece of sinew. And Robbie gave me a big kiss.

The entire group of settlers celebrated together, first in prayer, then eating four deer the men had managed to hunt over the last few days. Jasper McKay played his pipes and everyone sang "Auld Lang Syne."

We will leave soon to follow the Indians farther south. The Indians will follow the buffalo and we will follow the Indians.

January 8

I can only write when the sun is shining and there is no wind at all. Then the flap of the tent can be pulled back and I can sit by the fire, so my hands are warm enough and the ink does not freeze!

Our trip south was a repeat of our trek from The Forks to Pembina. We were not dressed for the weather. All I had was my tartan shawl wrapped around me, my warmest dress and my woollen stockings, but it was hardly sufficient against the bitter cold. There were times when I felt so cold I almost wept. Thank goodness Robbie was more protected than I.

When we arrived at our first camping ground nearer the buffalo herds we set up a small tent that Father had bought before we left. White Loon's family encouraged us to set up beside them. They have adopted us and are treating us rather like poor children who need help.

White Loon's family consists of a grandmother and grandfather, her mother and father, three brothers and a younger sister close to Robbie's age. The roles of our family became clear the first day the women of White Loon's family set up their large tipi. Father and James followed White Loon's father and brothers out to the hunt. Since it is the open plain they do not hunt the buffalo the same way as they did in Pembina, but rather race their horses beside the great beasts and shoot them with guns. Otherwise they try to manoeuvre them into snowbanks where they can be slowed down and more easily shot with arrows. Father, James and the other settlers had to drag the dead buffalo back to the camp. This took them over two days of backbreaking work.

In the meantime the women help with cooking, and Kate, Alice and I are sent out to dig up clods of grass and frozen buffalo turd, which is used in the fire. We are sent to the river for water and have to carry the heavy water skins back and forth. When the men returned with the buffalo they were put to work cutting and hauling wood.

January 18

I cannot believe how far from my dreams we have sunk. We were supposed to begin a life where I would be a lady. Instead I am nothing more than a servant to savages. I always try to bear myself with dignity, however, so as not to let them see that my pride is injured.

January 21

White Loon seems surprisingly sensitive to my state of mind, and right from the beginning has made an effort to soften the effects of her mother's orders. She takes every opportunity to speak with me and to learn our language, and she encourages me to do the same.

January 25

I must tell you, dear diary, something changed today. I hope, Mother, that you will not disapprove too much, although I fear that you will. You always wanted me to behave like a lady, and you prized that above all else. And so did I. Now I am not sure. In fact, I am in general rather confused. I think back to that reckless act on the ice floe when I behaved in a very unladylike way, and I wonder if I did not start down this dubious path then. But to the point.

The men had just finished a successful hunt, and the women had finished their work on the buffalo. The band seemed to decide it was time for some fun. The day had dawned bright and clear. There was a fresh fall of snow on the ground from the night before, which twinkled and sparkled in the sunlight. The sky was cloudless and blue. There was no wind, and although the temperature was very cold it seems that one can be outdoors as long as the bitter wind is absent. White Loon rushed into our tent, her eyes shining, her cheeks already red from being outdoors. She grabbed my hand and said, "You, come. Play."

I was so surprised that I did not protest and

went with her. I noticed that Kate, Alice and the other girls were already among the large group of women who had gathered near one end of the encampment. The women were moving to the centre, chatting and laughing. White Loon ran to the group, picked up something and ran back to me. She was holding two balls made of deerskin. The balls were connected to each other by a strip of hide. She pulled me back to the group and picked up a stick, which was lying on the ground. The stick was around 3 feet long and curved at one end. She threw the balls onto the stick, then lifted the stick into the air to show how the balls balanced on each side. She then lifted the stick and threw the balls off the stick, forward. She pointed to her hands and said, "No." Then she pointed to her feet and said, "No." Then she motioned for me to come and join her group. I noticed that Kate was already with the other group.

One of the women let out a small cry and the game began. It was obvious that we had to move the balls, but I had no idea where the goal was. Our team began with the balls on our sticks and the other team tried to pull them off our sticks with their own.

Suddenly White Loon threw the balls and they

landed on my stick. I was terribly nervous about what to do, but I had to do something and so I bolted ahead. I did not know exactly where I was going, but I was determined not to let the others grab the balls off my stick. Kate raced up and planted herself in front of me and attacked my stick with her own. She was also using her foot although that clearly was not allowed. Finally she was able to steal the balls from me and her team passed them back and forth between them until they reached the tipi at the far end of the clearing.

It was our team's turn again. The women began to pass the balls back and forth. They called to one another and taunted the other team. They began to pick up speed, running faster and throwing harder. White Loon ran with the stick and balls to a tipi at the other end of the clearing, and by her whooping and yipping I surmised that we had now scored a goal as well.

Then Kate had the balls again. I looked at her and decided she would not have them for long. Just as she was raising her stick to throw the balls, I looped them off with my stick, turned and threw to White Loon's mother, Leaf Bud, who ran with them to the tipi, scoring once again. I whooped and screamed with everyone else and then delved into the battle as fiercely as if it were a war. Time went so quickly that as the sky began to darken I realized we had spent the whole afternoon playing and that I could not remember a time when I had felt my blood pump through my heart and body with such a feeling of well-being.

This was certainly not the behaviour of a lady. I should have sat quietly in the tipi sewing or mending.

February 5

I have not been writing because when the days are clear and there is no wind I have taken every opportunity to play. I am now known among the women as the fiercest, most dangerous player of all the settlers, including Kate, who tried to keep up with me but was unable to. Even Father and James and Robbie took note as they watched some of our games. Father seemed happy I was enjoying myself and did not seem to notice my unladylike behaviour. Robbie was very proud of me.

February 9

It turns out that both Robbie and James are very good at games themselves. The boys play a game similar to ours, except that their ball is not a double but a single one. James is very good at driving the ball with his stick, which is what the men do instead of throwing it, but he is not as fearless as I and often has the ball stolen from him. No one steals the balls from me.

Robbie has become an expert at a sliding game. A strip of snow about 5 feet long is brushed off and iced down to make it slippery. At the end of the slope are small holes, around twelve of them. The tips of buffalo horns are rounded off to make little smooth stones and the young boys roll the stones down the slope, scoring points when they drop into the different holes. Robbie is patient and he concentrates fiercely. He and Peter often play together and have become quite a team. It seems our entire family has some kind of talent in the games.

February 12

I know that I should not be enjoying myself so much, and I fear that I am becoming a savage instead of helping the savages raise themselves up, but I cannot stop myself. I love the attention the other women give me and I love their praise. I simply try to put thoughts of Mother and her teachings aside. Sometimes it seems to be only harmless fun and nothing to be ashamed of, but at other times I know in my heart that it is wrong.

Kate has taken to tormenting me. "Is that the behaviour of a lady?" she squeals. "Oh my, look at Little Miss Manners now!" Fortunately we are not living in the same tent as she is, but I see her constantly anyway, as she is always somehow nearby. She is not to be got rid of.

February 19

It has been too windy to write. I have a moment on our first sunny day in a while — but only a moment. I must get to my chores. Still I want to relate how we have been spending our evenings.

Although the Indians don't read from books as we do, they tell stories at night around the campfire, and now, after a month or so, I find that I am able to understand little bits and pieces. They often seem to be about animals. They believe that certain animals watch over them and guide them. It does not sound that different to me than our angels, except all the animals have such different personalities and are so vivid that it almost seems more exciting than an angel, who appears boring in comparison. But there you see again, dear diary, how I began to sink into their world and to forget the superiority of my own.

February 22

I had just fallen into a deep sleep last night when I was suddenly awakened by loud shouting outside. I could not imagine who would be out making such noise in the middle of the night. Robbie ran out of the tent after pulling on his moccasins, and then ran right back in again.

"Come see, come see!" he shouted.

We all followed him outside. He pointed up. To the sky. The sky was flooded with lights of all different shades and hues, just like a rainbow, but at night!

"Ghost dancers," White Loon said.

"No, no," Father corrected her. "It is *aurora borealis.*"

It was beautiful and I was in awe at the sight. We stood there as long as we could until the cold drove us back to the warmth of our tents and blankets.

March 3

A fresh load of buffalo was dragged into camp by the men after another successful hunt a few weeks ago, and there has been no time to write since then. The women and girls work very hard when the buffalo first come into camp, and we settlers were put to work right along with the Indian women. I shall describe here what we do:

First we cut the meat into very thin spiral strips and hang it on racks. But last week the weather was too snowy and wet so it was hung inside the tipi. Four poles are supported by a platform that is set up over the fire. The smell is so strong that at first I had to choose between staying warm in the tipi, being alone in our own tent, or freezing yet being able to breathe outside. But the temperature has plummeted and my skin began to freeze after only minutes. Quickly it was no longer a choice — I simply had to get used to the smell.

When the meat was finally dry we tied it up and stored it in rawhide sacks. After a few days passed we took it out and pounded it with stone hammers. The first time that I helped with this work my arms were so sore the next morning I could barely lift them. After the meat was pounded to a pulp we added berries and then poured buffalo fat over it all. This was allowed to set and then packed again in hides. When it was all done, I felt a great sense of accomplishment, knowing we had just made pemmican for weeks to come.

But our work was not over. Next the hides needed to be tanned. Leaf Bud led the work, as White Loon's grandmother was not well. First Leaf Bud simmered the brains, liver and fat of a buffalo calf in water. This she made into a soft paste. That is when we girls were put to work.

We rubbed the paste all over the hide. It was dried by the fire for days, and again the smell was overwhelming. Then we soaked it in water and rolled it all into a bundle, only to unroll it again, stretch it out and rub it with our hands. For days we rubbed until my hands were so sore it hurt just to open and close my fingers. But on the final day Leaf Bud gave me a piece of the hide so I could make a skirt from it. The one I'd been wearing was in tatters and so it was a welcome gift — and yet was it? Could I wear it and not seem just like one of them? And is that a good or a bad thing?

March 10

Weather has been cold, too cold to write. I plan to wait until we return to Pembina before I write again.

March 21

We have returned! There is a thaw in the weather appropriate to the first day of spring, and I find myself quite comfortable wrapped in my tartan shawl. I am determined to make up for the long absence in these pages and will try to be more dependable in my writing. In a way I am glad to be back to the relative comfort of Fort Daer, but I already miss the fun we had living with the Indians, if not the backbreaking work. And, of course, Kate and her father are living with us again, and Kate is as bothersome as ever.

March 22

I am sitting by the fire writing because I feel so helpless I do not know what else to do. James went out hunting with White Loon's brothers. Late this afternoon the sky suddenly darkened. White Loon came by our cabin and said there was a big storm coming and that she hoped the boys would be safe.

I went outside with her and gazed at the sky. It was dark and a wind was blowing up from the north. It bit at my cheeks and I could feel the temperature dropping even as we stood there. "Are they in danger?" I asked her.

She shrugged and said, "It will be bad."

I ran to find Father, who was just returning from a trip to the small store. He had a large bag and he smiled when he saw me and said, "Oatmeal." I was glad to see that he was regaining his sense of humour — oatmeal, was, after all, the only thing we had to eat besides what the men could hunt, but he held it up as if it were gold. I hated to worry him, but I had no choice.

"Father, White Loon says a storm is brewing and James has gone out hunting with her brothers."

Father's face fell and he looked at White Loon as if she could make the bad weather disappear. She hurried over to him and spoke softly and his face seemed to relax a bit, as if she had said something to make him feel better. I wish I knew what it was because I feel no less anxious. I suspect it was only her manner that reassured him — perhaps she said something about her brothers and how they have survived worse than this.

The storm blew in a few hours later and now we are shut up, trembling at its power. Outside, you cannot see your hand in front of your face. And inside, the wind howls through the cracks in the wood so fiercely that I am forced to end this writing as the pages of the diary are flapping even as I try to hold them down. I pray for James and, of course, for White Loon's brothers.

March 23

It is my birthday. Father and White Loon gave me a beautiful Indian necklace. My only wish is to have James home safely. All celebrations are forgotten.

Evening

No news. The storm worsens, if that could be possible. How will they survive?

March 24

Daybreak. No change. The wind continues to howl. We almost froze even with the fire going all night. Dread fills me.

Afternoon

We have been reading from the Bible and praying.

Kate is past annoying. She babbles on and on about James being foolhardy enough to go out with savages. They are his only hope. Can she not see that?

Evening

Still nothing and the storm rages on unabated.

March 25

I awoke this morning to an eerie silence, the likes of which I have never experienced. We all stirred at about the same time. I would not have known it was morning except for the fact that I could see a little stream of light coming in through the cracks in the wood. Father said he would go ask White Loon's father, Black Bear, if he knew anything about the hunters. I suspect he was anxious to get out and form a party to go looking for them. But when he went to open the door it would not open, not an inch. He threw his weight against it and so did Kate's father (who had managed to spend two days with us without saying more than two words). Still it would not budge.

We were trapped by the snow.

"We will just have to wait patiently," Father said. "I'm sure the Indians will be able to get out of their tipis, as they have no wooden doors to stop them. And they will be able to travel on their snowshoes. We must hope that they will dig us out."

It was a horrible wait. I made oatmeal for everyone. We ate, but said little and spoke little. We were too worried about James. Even Kate managed to hold her tongue, perhaps realizing that no one would have patience with her today. And as each minute passed I felt more and more hemmed in until at times I felt like screaming.

Finally we thought we heard something. It was as if our hut were really a cocoon because it was so quiet we could barely hear, but at last it was apparent that there were definite sounds of scraping. I could see the snow was being cleared as more and more light broke through the cracks. And then there were sounds by the door. Finally the door opened just a bit. And then inch by inch it was pulled outward. John Lawson and Peter MacDonald stood there, faces red with exertion. Just behind them were a number of the men from the Indian band. We all ran to the door and peered out.

What a sight! The sun hurt my eyes so much at first that I could barely see. Father wrapped himself in a blanket and went to join the men in order to dig out the other huts. Black Bear was among the Indians and I saw Father go over to speak to him. Father's face fell. He looked back at me and shook his head. No news.

If I had not known there was a settlement around me I could never have guessed. The snow had drifted up to the rooftops in places. Indians were travelling on snowshoes, but each time Father took a step he sank well over his knees, sometimes up to his waist, and had to be pulled ahead by Black Bear. They were trying to make small trails from one hut to another, but they had to do it with their hands and the rough shovels that the Indians brought. Kate and I pulled the door shut. I sit by the fire and wait.

I realize I have not written very much in these pages about James and that I have been terribly remiss not to do so. It is just that he is such a good brother that I have few complaints about him. I now recognize how much I have taken his presence for granted. While I have tried to take on Mother's role, in many ways James has taken on Father's, for Father is often too sunk in grief to do the things a father normally does. On that most difficult trip from York Factory it was always James who exhorted us to carry on, who tried to take our fatigue away by making jokes, and by kind words when they were necessary. James never seemed afraid. But that is not to say he is not refined. He will never show me the poetry he writes that I know he keeps secret. Sometimes he will recite one of his finer pieces, but only if he thinks it is fit to be listened to. He does not like to fight, that is sure. And some boys think he is less of a man for it, but I think he is more of a man.

I know one thing to be true. Father could not survive one more loss. I am not sure I could either.

Evening

James is alive! He was carried into the hut by Black Bear just as evening drew near. He could not walk by himself because he is blind! I have wrapped him up and fed him oatmeal and hot tea. I notice that his ears are white and that worries me too, as I do not know what it means. Father has led us all in a prayer thanking God for James's return.

March 27

Alice's mother has managed to make her way over here by one of the small trails the men have dug out in between the huts. Father went to fetch her in the hope that she could help James. She says that his blindness will disappear. It is called snow blindness and is not a lasting affliction. She's more worried about his ears and has told us that the white means that they were frozen and he must always keep them protected from the cold from now on so as not to develop an infection. James has slept and slept and has not yet been able to tell us what happened.

March 28

I shall try to write down as closely as possible James's account as he described his harrowing adventure. He and White Loon's three brothers, Fire Owl, Jumps and Small Beaver, all decided to go out on their own for a hunt. They were not looking for buffalo but rather for deer and to set traps for rabbits. James had become friends with these three boys just as I had become a friend of White Loon's. Fire Owl and Jumps are older — closer to the age of White Loon, but Small Beaver seems to be close to James's age. He and James spend much time together and James is becoming familiar with their language.

They began tracking a family of deer and they moved farther and farther away from the camp. James did notice the sky was beginning to darken, and he believes Small Beaver did as well, for he spoke to his older brothers about it, but they were intent on the hunt and did not listen. The wind began to blow up, the snow began to fall, and the deer tracks were becoming harder and harder to follow. It was then that the brothers realized that they had to get back to camp. But the storm came on so quickly it soon became apparent they would never reach camp by nightfall, or rather the storm would reach them before they reached camp. The boys knew that there was a small cluster of trees not too far distant and it was to this that they made their way.

It was almost dark when they arrived. Quickly they pulled down branches from the trees and stoked a fire, but within hours the wind had picked up to such a degree the fire could not hold. They lay flat under the trees and covered themselves with branches for what little protection they offered. They remained there in that spot all that night, all the next day, and all the next night. The wind did not hold steady but picked up and dropped off, and whenever possible they started a fire. They were sure that is what saved their lives — a few hours or even minutes of warmth. When the storm ended and the day dawned bright and clear they tried to walk home, but were weak from not eating, and every step they took they sank into the snow. By the time

Black Bear found them James assured us he could not have taken one more step. His eyesight was almost gone and Jumps was leading him. Small Beaver was also affected and could not see. Black Bear had brought snowshoes for them, but imagine how difficult it is to walk on them in the first place, and in the second place to walk on them without your sight.

And here despite the gravity of the situation James soon had us all roaring with laughter as he described himself blind and stumbling on his snowshoes, Jumps and Fire Owl mercilessly teasing both him and Small Beaver, probably to encourage them to go on.

April 5

I have had no time to write as I have been nursing James. At night I read to him rather than write in your pages. The weather continues sunny, but bitterly cold. We can now travel between huts, but we are getting very short on food because the hunters cannot get out. And the store is almost out of all provisions except oatmeal.

April 8

As I was sitting with Alice at her hut sewing I overheard her mother and father talking about the North West Company and their plans to drive the settlers away from The Forks again. Apparently Colin Robertson, who took charge of Alice's group after they were driven away from Red River, approached Duncan Cameron in February and told him to stop spreading rumours that would frighten the settlers — as he had done so successfully before, scaring away all but these thirteen hardy families. It seemed at first that Duncan Cameron was amenable to his suggestions, but as the months went by that assumption proved to be untrue. Only a month ago, in March, Duncan Cameron returned to Fort Gibraltar wearing his British regimentals and boasted that he could drive the settlers out once again. That means us. (Have I mentioned, dear diary, that Fort Gibraltar was the North West fort near Fort Douglas, also at the junction of the Red and Assiniboine rivers?)

So Colin Robertson decided to seize Fort Gibraltar. He confiscated all the correspondence he found there. In Cameron's correspondence he discovered letters from the North West Company urging the Métis to attack all of us. In particular there was a letter that talked of uniting the Métis to drive their enemy — us — from the land. On the basis of these letters Robertson arrested Duncan Cameron there.

Apparently Colin Robertson believes that when we return to The Forks we should stay at Fort Douglas for our own protection, but Governor Semple disagrees and believes we will be safe to go and farm the land. It is true that some of the men have learned how to handle guns this winter when they were hunting, but they have never fought. How would we defend ourselves?

Alice and I looked at each other. I wanted to ask questions, but it was obvious that we should not even have overheard and that the adults did not want to discuss this with the children. When I got home later I questioned Father about all of this and asked him why he had not told us anything.

"I did not want to worry you," he replied. "You are only children."

"But we deserve to know, Father," James objected.

"Frankly," Father said, "I believe Colin Robertson has a better idea of the politics and the dangers that we are encountering than Governor

Semple does. In the letters Colin Robertson has been sending to us he refers to the Governor as Mr. Simple, and I begin to fear that he is right — and yet our fate seems to be in Semple's hands."

It appeared to me that Father had gone from not telling us enough, to telling us too much. Now I really am worried. If we cannot trust the judgement of our Governor there is reason to worry.

April 10

White Loon has taken to coming to our hut at night so she can hear me read from the Bible. She speaks a funny combination of Gaelic, learned from the other settlers, and English learned from me during our time on the prairie. Sometimes I see her talking to Father during the day as the chores are done. She can actually make him laugh. I never thought I would see him laugh again. But this confuses me, just as my time with the Indians was confusing. If she is such a savage, why is she so nice? Are Indians only savages because they do not accept the Bible? I thought they would be bloodthirsty killers, not to be trusted, but they are not that at all.

I will ask Father.

April 12

Father says that the Indians have a culture that is very old. He says he learned much about it when we were living so close to them, especially when he went hunting with the Indian men. At night the Indians would sit around the campfire and tell stories. Father asked many questions, and they were happy to answer them. I asked Father about Indians and the Bible. He said we could teach them. He said that it is not their fault that they are ignorant of the teachings of the Bible, and just as I am educating White Loon, so would others be educated.

"But what if they don't want to be educated?" I asked him.

"Then they will choose not to be," he answered. "It will be up to them."

In the meantime he seems more worried about the Nor'Westers than these questions about the Indians. He worries that Governor Semple will not listen to Colin Robertson and that we might be in danger. He says that soon we will be moving back to The Forks. I cannot wait! Finally we will be able to build our own little house and truly begin our lives in the New Land. The weather is warming considerably, but there is so much snow that no one wants it to get too warm too quickly, or we may find ourselves in the midst of quite a flood. The Indians tell tales of such a thing and seem quite fearful of it.

April 15

Father told us more tonight as we ate our dinner. Apparently Duncan Cameron and the other Nor' Westers — after Colin Robertson captured them at Fort Gibraltar — were transported to Fort Douglas. And Mr. Robertson wants to send Duncan Cameron and the correspondence that proves he is out to harm us back to England, for trial. He also wants to unite the camps of Fort Douglas and Fort Gibraltar, and he wants us to remain at one of the Forts and not go back to the land. But Governor Semple disagrees, and will send us onto the land.

Father looked firmly at Robbie. "Now lad," he said, "I know you will be tempted to run and play with your Indian friends, but you must not stray too far away from our land at any time." Robbie grinned. He had the look of one who had no intention of *not* running and playing.

April 20

I barely know how to write this or what to say. I almost think that if I do not write it, Mother will not find out, but I know that you are looking down, Mother, and that you already know. But what a shock to me. And to James and Robbie.

Father intends to marry White Loon!

I am at such a loss I cannot put another word down.

April 21

It is true. I spoke to White Loon.

April 23

I have been in a daze. I cannot think straight.

April 24

I struck Kate. And she began to cry. She had said something horrible about Father — that he was marrying a savage. She and her father have moved into a different hut.

April 25

Alice sits with me constantly and lets me talk and talk. Her mother has been very kind and tells me not to be so hard on Father. She reminds me how much I liked White Loon until this happened. And she points out all the other marriages similar to this — the Métis, after all, are a large number of people. James has taken to sitting with us too, and Alice makes sure that she is very sympathetic to him. Robbie seems unaffected. He likes White Loon and says he will be glad to have a mother.

"But I am your mother," I objected.

"No, you are my sister," he said.

April 28

We are making preparations to leave. James Sutherland, the Church elder who performed the first marriages, is to perform this ceremony before we go, so that White Loon will be part of our family by the time we return to The Forks.

Evening

White Loon and I had a long talk this afternoon. We speak in a mixture of English and Cree, but naturally I cannot write the Cree down here so I will write it all as if it were in English.

"We are friends, Isobel, yes?" she asked.

"I thought we were . . ." I answered. "But how could you be my friend," I blurted out, "when you are taking my father away?"

She looked at me for a long time and then took my hand. "No," she said, softly, "I give him back to you."

I stared at her. "Do you mean you won't marry him after all?"

She shook her head, obviously searching for words. "I mean he is not happy alone. He needs a wife. When he has a wife he will be a good father again, happy."

"But I have been taking care of him," I snapped. "He doesn't need anyone else. He has a family and we keep together and take care of one another."

She nodded. "You are *too* good. You work hard all day. The only time you played was when we were on the prairie with the buffalo. And then you were happy. You are still young. Too young to be a mother. Be a good hardworking daughter. That is enough."

"I have a mother," I grumbled.

"Then I will not be your mother." She smiled.

"I will be your friend, as always. And with James, he maybe is too old for another mother. But Robbie is not. And your father is too young to be without a wife."

Then I realized that I have been thinking only of myself, not of Father at all. He is happy now, but why was I not enough to make him happy? I still cannot seem to accept this.

April 30

This afternoon my father married White Loon. It was a beautiful warm day. There are still a few inches of snow on the ground, which proved beneficial for the ceremony because beneath the snow is only mud. Instead of a muddy miserable place, Fort Daer looked at its best today. It is true the snow is no longer white, rather a pale grey, but there was a definite smell and feel of spring.

The entire settlement turned out for the ceremony. The Indians also attended, bringing fresh meat. The ceremony was held outside. After it was over we ate and Jasper McKay played at the pipes. Everyone danced. I could not. White Loon asked me to stand up with her but I refused. Her mother and Alice stood with her. Robbie and James stood with Father. After the celebrations had been going on for a while White Loon and Father left for a short trip away on their own. They will be back in two days. Meanwhile James is in charge of the family.

I feel nothing. The entire day went by as if I were in a dream. Why am I — and Kate — the only one who thinks this is so wrong? Father tried to speak to me many times over the last few days, but I had nothing to say to him.

What should I say? You betrayed my mother? You betrayed me?

May 2

Father and White Loon have returned and now, of course, White Loon is living with us. I must admit that already she is taking a large burden from me. I have never wanted to complain in these pages, especially as I feel I am writing to Mother as well as to myself, and I wouldn't want to blame Mother in any way for leaving me in charge, but it has been difficult taking care of Father and two boys all by myself. I must clean the cabin, cook, sew and mend and somehow take care of Robbie's education. It is this latter task that has suffered the most. Robbie spends all his time with his friends, playing, and no time at all with his studies. I have been very worried about this. But now White Loon has taken over the cooking and only needs me to help with the cleaning, which gives me time to spend with Robbie. I suppose this is a good thing. She is as friendly as ever and does not seem to resent me for my ungracious behaviour. If I were her I would be furious with me. Father is smiling and making jokes. He still wishes to speak to me. I may have to speak to him. We leave in two days for The Forks.

May 3

James has sat me down and given me a talking to. "You are behaving like a child," he said to me. "Father loves White Loon."

"Why did he stop loving Mother so quickly?" I asked.

"Of course he hasn't," James replied. "He will always love Mother. But she will never come back. I thought you liked White Loon."

"I did until I found out she was after Father," I replied.

James laughed. "She was never after him," he said. "Oh, you're too young to understand."

I am not too young!

May 4

Tomorrow we start our trip back to The Forks. I will not be able to write again until we arrive. Robbie is riding back with one of White Loon's brothers. He's so excited he can barely contain himself. The rest of us will walk.

May 15

We have been staying at Fort Douglas in a tent ever since we arrived back at The Forks. And we have been building the new cabin. I often find myself just standing and looking out over the prairie where we will soon finally have our home. We had to leave so quickly in the winter that I never saw where we would live and now it is a wonderful surprise. Father says this land is perfect for farming, and the settlers who left for Upper Canada had already begun clearing it.

I remember the feelings I had on the ship of being closed in, and I rejoice that I shall never feel that again, for the land seems to go on forever. There are trees, naturally, which break up the vista, but I can sense the expanse around me. Sometimes I feel like running and running and running, my face in the warm wind, knowing that nothing will stop me. Land stretches out around me so that I could run for weeks and never have to stop!

Today we built the chimney for our house. White Loon's brothers have been helping us, and once the chimney is finished we will finally be able to move in. First the framework was built of branches. This was held together with a paste made of clay, water and straw. This hardens almost immediately and when we start a fire it will become harder and harder — as good as bricks.

But let me tell you a little of that trip back to our new home.

As we walked the prairie seemed to explode in colour around us. There were crocuses everywhere, the colour of the blue sky. Trees and bushes that would bear fruit in a couple of months were covered in blossoms — small white sweet-smelling wild plums, saskatoon bushes, chokecherries and pin cherries — Alice naming them for me as we walked. She also pointed out the strawberry plants and the raspberry and blueberry bushes. The trees appeared to come into leaf as we walked: oak, elm, poplar, cotton-wood, ash, maple. The colour of the leaves was a striking young green. It was as if the entire world around us was in a frenzy of excitement crying Spring! Spring! I saw a beautiful red-breasted bird, and there were many red-winged black-birds, as well as yellow finches, meadowlarks with their beautiful song, and bluejays with their striking markings and horrible squawking.

I concentrated on the wonders about me, walked with Alice, and tried to ignore my family as much as possible. Kate seemed to decide that she was unwilling to stop bothering me just because of Father's unsuitable marriage, so the only seeming benefit from that disappeared. She was back to pestering me! She often walked with Alice and me, teasing me and taunting me about White Loon whenever she could, until I found myself defending White Loon and Father.

It seems that we have certainly gained another family. Jumps took Robbie on his horse, and James was able to travel with Small Beaver. The boys found this terribly exciting. At night we often ate with White Loon's family at their tipi and if we made camp early we would be included in the games played just before the sun set.

The game played most by the girls as we trav-elled was a stick game. Two digging sticks were placed about a foot apart. The girls would stand a few yards back and throw other digging sticks, trying to get them to land in between the two sticks placed in the dirt. Even when we walked the girls would play — they would just pick any target, a bush or tree, and see who could hit it with a stick. White Loon encouraged Alice and me to play, and as with the other games I discovered I was very good at it. And as before, I loved the feeling of being good at something and the generous way the other girls applauded my skill.

If the fireplace is deemed to be built correctly we can move into our new cabin within days.

May 17

There has been an attack on a Hudson's Bay Company trader by a man named Cuthbert Grant. He is a Métis leader and a member of the North West Company. Father says that the Nor'Westers dressed like Indians in war paint, and stole all the furs in the trader's shipment.

Now Governor Semple *has* to listen to Colin Robertson about the threat posed by the North West Company. Father hopes he will finally authorize Mr. Robertson to take Duncan Cameron to England for trial on the grounds of treason, using those dreadful letters threatening the colony as proof. Father is terribly worried. Colin Robertson is the only sensible leader, and Father wonders what may happen without his good advice while he's away in England. Mr. Robertson is still in command of Fort Gibraltar, the Nor'Westers' Fort, and it seems he will stay there for the present.

May 25

I know I have written very little, but there is no time. We moved into our own cabin a week ago and have been so busy that I simply go to sleep at night before I can pick up my pen. Father has put me in charge of the garden, but we had a dreadful time obtaining our seeds. We went to ·the Company store, set up temporarily in a room in the Fort, and were treated terribly. Father says he may as well still be back in the Highlands to be spoken to that way. It took us two days at the store, going from one official to another and spoken to as if we were lowly servants, until we finally obtained the seed we need: beans, potatoes, carrots and turnips.

The garden is wonderful work but exhausting. But the black flies are particularly bad. I am covered in bites. We take mud from the river and slather it on. White Loon has made a salve and that helps. Poor Robbie is quite covered in bites. We also have to check for wood ticks every night and then White Loon burns them off with a small branch she sets on fire, and blows out just before sticking it on a creature. They are nasty, as they dig right into your flesh.

Father is planting oats and wheat. Oh, I am remiss! I have not described our little bit of land here.

Our plot runs straight back from the river. There is a rough road, or track really, connecting all the farms to the Fort. There is a natural windbreak of poplar. By the river are the most beautiful willows whose branches reach all the way to the ground. Father was able to begin ploughing right away. Unfortunately there are not enough ploughs for all the farmers, so everyone has to share.

May 26

Father and a number of the other men have gone to visit Colin Robertson at Fort Gibraltar. The men believe we settlers should stay with him at the Fort until the danger has passed. Every day there are more and more rumours of Métis plotting to destroy our colony. Everyone is worried.

May 27

It has been raining for two days and we have been stuck indoors together. (I will not complain again about how I long to be released.) I have had to converse with White Loon. It would be rude to do otherwise, placed together like this for hours on end. As we talked I remembered our friendship, and my heart softened toward her just a little. But I still cannot seem to accept Father's betrayal of Mother nor White Loon's new position in the house as wife and mistress. It is true she has not abused her position. She does not order me to do things. What would happen if I did question her organization of the household? And is giving in and liking her just more of what Kate keeps taunting me about — am I becoming a savage myself? Is it not up to me to retain the standards of our old life? Do I not still want to become a lady?

June 2

Very disturbing news today. A group of Métis disguised as Indians attacked Brandon House, a Hudson's Bay Company post north of here. There were approximately forty or fifty men and they flew the new Métis flag — a square of red with a figure eight lying sideways in the centre. They ransacked the Post, forcing all the families to take shelter with the Cree Indians. Nobody was killed, but all the pemmican and tobacco and liquor and ammunition were taken. Father fears the ammunition will be used against us. We're all very worried. We wonder if we should not go live in the Fort. But Governor Semple will not allow us to and insists that we stay on the land and continue to farm. Every day when I go out to work in the garden I find myself looking around nervously, wondering if a band of painted men will ride down upon us and kill me and my family as we stand. Alice too is worried, and Kate seems the most worried of all. Although she must have her own work to do on her own farm, I often find her simply standing there beside me as I garden.

June 9

This morning Jumps rode up to our cabin in such a manner that my heart leapt into my throat. He spoke quickly with White Loon and by the expression on her face I knew that the news must be bad. Without speaking to me she ran to find Father in the field. She came back shaking her head with worry. Apparently the Indians say there is a large group coming down the Assiniboine with the sole purpose of destroying our colony. Jumps has ridden to the Fort to pass the news on to Governor Semple.

June 10

Governor Semple has ordered Fort Gibraltar to be stripped and the palisades floated downriver to be used to protect Fort Douglas. Colin Robertson still believes that we settlers should be moved into Fort Douglas for our own protection. Governor Semple will hear none of it. Father says the two men had a huge fight and Mr. Robertson has decided to leave, saying he cannot stay in the same place as Governor Semple. This is a terrible outcome, as Colin Robertson seems to be the only sensible person here. Father warns us all to stay near the cabin and to watch closely if we're out in the fields or near the river. But we still have to be outdoors all day working, so it is nerve-wracking to say the least.

June 16

An Indian named Moustache has arrived this morning in Fort Douglas. He says he escaped from the Métis camp at Portage la Prairie. He says there is a heavily armed party of Métis and some Indians that will be here within two days. Chief Peguis, who is the Chief of the Saulteaux Indians — the one Alice says helped the settlers over the last two winters — has offered to help us now. But Governor Semple has declined. He must be mad!

June 19

I write with trembling hand. We are at present virtual prisoners in Fort Douglas. But let me go back a little and relate the terrible events of the last few hours.

White Loon decided just after tea to go to the river to pull in her fish nets. She asked me to go with her as Father was going to the fields with the boys to do the weeding. I had been planning to write in your pages, dear diary, but White Loon convinced me to take you with me, so I could sit under a tree by the river and write there. It seemed a pleasant proposal so I agreed.

We set off and were delighted to discover that one net was filled with fish. Just as we were pulling it in she motioned me to stop and put her fingers to her lips. She had obviously heard something. I began to feel the ground rumbling. White Loon pulled me down beneath a large willow tree. My heart was in my throat. Were we about to be attacked? Where were Father and my brothers?

"We must go warn the men," I said to her.

"No," she said firmly, holding onto me. "It is too dangerous. The horses are coming this way."

"We should have stayed in the Fort as Colin Robertson wanted," I said. "What will happen now?"

She shushed me then as the pounding of horses' hooves grew louder. We were by a bend in the river. Beyond our hiding place were numerous tall oak trees in full leaf — the reason the place is called Seven Oaks. Beyond that is a small open space called Frog Plain.

And then they were there — a band of men who looked like Indians to me because their faces were smeared with paint of the most bright and frightening variety. But White Loon whispered to me, "Those are not my brothers; those are mixed bloods."

"Métis?" I whispered.

She nodded.

Later I learned the watchman from the Fort had seen them coming. Governor Semple decided to go meet them and talk to them.

Very shortly we saw the Governor's party

advance. It seemed there were about twenty men with him.

"Is Father amongst them?" I whispered.

"I do not see him," she answered, "but I see Kate's father, and Alice's father too."

A man rode out from the trees where they had been waiting on horseback and called to the Governor's party, "What do you want?"

"What do *you* want?" the Governor called back.

"We want our Fort."

"Go to your Fort!" the Governor called.

He couldn't mean Fort Gibraltar — the North West Company fort — I thought, as that had been dismantled. I could not quite understand *what* he meant. But then the other man shouted, "Why did you destroy our Fort, you damned rascal?"

The two men drew near to each other, the Governor on foot, the other man on his horse. We were close enough to see Governor Semple's face go all red — furious, most likely, that a man not of his station could speak to him in such a manner. Suddenly the Governor reached out his hands and grabbed the reins of the other's horse. Just then more Métis rode in from behind the Governor's party, so they were cut off and surrounded.

And then a shot rang out. I could not see who had fired first. White Loon threw herself over me and for the next while — I do not know how long although it felt like an eternity — we remained frozen. There was the horrible sound of men crying out in pain, shots fired, men shouting to one another and general chaos and mayhem. I clearly heard the Governor's voice as he begged for his life, saying he was not mortally wounded should they fetch the surgeon. But there was more gunfire and then his voice fell silent.

I finally pushed White Loon's hand away in time to see Alice's father and another man I did not recognize running low to the ground from tree to tree so that the Métis would not notice them. They passed so close to where we were hiding we could have touched them as they ran past us. I prayed to God that they would escape. I heard a splash of water, and saw that they were paddling toward the Fort, keeping close to the bank.

Finally, after what felt like hours, as the sky began to darken White Loon said, "We must go to the Fort. I think the men have gone. Do not look over there. You will see only death." She took my hand. "Now, while we have the chance."

When I stood my legs crumpled beneath me. She had to support me. But I reminded myself that Mother always taught me to be unafraid and I determined that these murderers would not make me cower for one more minute. So I held her hand and we ran along the river, travelling to the Fort that way rather than along the road.

When we reached the Fort the first person I saw was Father, waiting by the gates. When he saw us his entire countenance was flooded with relief. White Loon and I ran into his arms.

"Are my brothers safe?" I gasped.

Yes," he replied, "safe here with me." He hurried us toward the large building where everyone was gathered. "Where have you been? We've been so worried!"

"We were by the river," I said. Then I stopped and turned to White Loon. "You took good care of me," I said. "Thank you."

She smiled and her whole face brightened.

"You are my daughter, sister. I will always take care of you and your family."

"Your brothers have come looking for you," Father said to White Loon. "Jumps is inside. Jeb Connor has just returned, soaking wet and telling terrible tales of a massacre."

I was happy to hear that Alice's father had made it back safely.

Father continued. "We saw the Métis coming and I hurried the boys to the Fort. We could not find you anywhere."

"We were right there, Father," I said. "We were hidden under a willow right by Seven Oaks. The Governor is dead. So are the others with him."

"Kate's father is one of them, I fear. She has just been told," Father said.

He hurried us into the main room where all the settlers were crammed together. Kate saw me, ran to me, grabbed me and began to sob and sob. I comforted her as best I could, surprised by this display of grief by a girl who had never expressed anything but scorn and contempt for all things, and whom I rarely saw say a word to her father or vice versa.

She lies by me now, sleeping at my feet as I write, exhausted by her tears. Father managed to find me ink and a pen, and my diary seems undamaged, which is fortunate considering that I was lying on it for so long.

The men are meeting, led now by the Sheriff, Alexander McDonell. They seem to have decided to defend Fort Douglas. We will not budge from here easily, not by the sound of the men.

June 20

Chief Peguis and his men have brought some of the bodies of those massacred back to the fort to be buried. Kate's father is one of them and at least she can see him put in the ground. There will be a brief service shortly.

Afternoon

Cuthbert Grant, the leader of the Métis, has sent a message saying that if we do not surrender the Fort we will all be murdered! It is said that the North West Company recently appointed this Cuthbert Grant as Captain General of all the half-breeds in the country. The man who brings this news is a Hudson's Bay man called John Pritchard who survived the massacre.

Robbie finds this all very exciting and wants to go and fight. James takes part in the deliberations with the older men. Alice weeps constantly, as does Kate, who will not leave my side, but I will not! I will not be afraid! I will not!

June 21

John Pritchard has circulated a petition encouraging capitulation. Father is furious. But most feel the threat of murder must be taken seriously, so almost all of the settlers have signed. Alexander McDonell agrees with Father, but they are in a minority and no one will listen. So the Sheriff has sent a message surrendering the Fort. Father rails against it, saying we have the big gun, they do not and we are in a Fort that cannot easily be breached.

June 22

I barely slept last night. Today Hudson's Bay Company officials are making an inventory of everything here before handing the Fort over to the Métis. The women and children are still weeping over loved ones lost. Kate seems inconsolable.

Later

I've told Father that we must adopt Kate. I know that this is strange because I do not even like her, and although she sticks to me like a leech she does not seem to like me either, but who else does she have? White Loon agrees, saying Kate is not nice just as many little sisters are not nice — that is the way of little sisters. James does not seem too happy at the prospect, nor does Robbie, who says that she is "grouchy."

June 23

Cuthbert Grant has gone back on his word and now says we cannot leave. He wants us to wait for officials of the North West Company from Qu'Appelle.

Later

Sheriff McDonell met with Cuthbert Grant and told him that if we wait for the officials from Qu'Appelle they will get credit for the victory over the Hudson's Bay Company. Grant wants the credit, so he's allowing us to leave. It was clever of the Sheriff to play on his vanity in such a way.

We must leave today. We go to Hudson Bay and — I can barely believe this, never mind write it — back to our homeland. What grief this is to bear. Our little cabin will be burned, my garden will be destroyed. All Mother's dreams for us, all the hardships we have endured — all for nothing?

How could this happen?

June 24

We have departed. I sit by the fire. I can write only a few words. We set off in eight boats, taking what little we were able. Father and White Loon hurried back to the cabin and salvaged what they could, packing two of our trunks. Just like my hands when they become too cold, my feelings have become the same. Numb.

June 26

We were stopped by a group of Nor'Westers today. And what an unusual number of events, both amazing and frightening, then ensued. We saw their brigade boats coming toward us on the river, sails hoisted. Their sails were quickly lowered and they put to shore. As we drew parallel to them they called to us to stop and demanded that we put to shore as well. They did this with guns raised. We had no choice but to follow their orders. We did not know what fate would befall us at their hands and I had to force myself to try to stay calm. We had not negotiated with them and we did not have the protection of the Fort. Father muttered under his breath, "We should have stayed where we were protected. Did I not say so?" As we came close to the shore Kate exclaimed, "William! It is William!"

"William?" I repeated.

"My brother," Kate said, eyes shining. "It is my brother!" And then I remembered that she did have a brother working for the North West Company, although she rarely spoke of him. Even when her father died she did not mention him, but perhaps she was afraid to remind us that her brother was a Nor'Wester after they had murdered so many of our people. Perhaps she herself was torn about his allegiance. But at that moment all those worries must have been set aside because her eyes glowed and tears threatened. As we pulled into shore she was one of the first to leap from the boat.

"William! William!" she called.

A young man turned around at the sound of her voice. "Kate!" he cried.

She ran over to him and then suddenly stopped as if she were about to throw her arms about him, but realized she could not. He put his hands on her shoulders and said something to her, which I could not hear. At that point she replied, speaking quickly, and then she seemed to crumple and he did put his arms about her. He helped her to a large log nearby and sat down with her, taking her hands in his. He was a tall lanky fellow whose ears stood out quite remarkably from a long thin face. But his manner seemed kind and I was very happy that Kate should find him.

In the meantime we were told by those in charge, very brusquely, to get out of the boats, to pitch our tents, and to bring all our belongings onto land.

In a low voice Father said to us, "They are looking for the correspondence that Colin Robertson obtained when he captured Duncan Cameron. It clearly shows the intent of the Nor'Westers to destroy our settlement, and would be damning in a court of law in England. Colin Robertson took a few pieces with him, but he left the majority at Fort Douglas, and the Nor'Westers are suspicious that we have brought it with us. If it is here anywhere we must hope they do not find it."

We unpacked the boats, then pitched our tent in a small clearing near the river, after which we lugged our trunks and belongings to the tent.

"My name is Archibald McLeod," said a stocky man with a very large voice. "Who is in charge here?"

Sheriff McDonell stepped forward. "I am, sir," he said. "Sheriff Alexander McDonell. And to what do we owe the pleasure of your company?"

At this Archibald McLeod's face grew very red and he exclaimed, "We will search all your belongings, sir."

Sheriff McDonell made a small low bow. This seemed to enrage their leader even more and he quickly ordered his men to start examining our things. They began to rummage through all of our trunks. They ascertained which was Governor Semple's trunk, broke the lock and thoroughly searched it as well.

As all this was going on Kate brought her brother over to meet us. "This is William," she said, and then introduced each of us to him.

"Kate has told me how well you have taken care of her," William said to us, "and I find myself forever in your debt." He looked very distraught. "I have just now learned of my father's death. Unfortunately I have signed a contract with the North West Company for another two years, and will not be able to leave to take care of her. She tells me that you have offered to do so." He paused and looked questioningly at Father.

"Yes," Father agreed, "we have and are most happy to do so."

Well, I thought to myself, perhaps we are not *happy* to do so, but what else can we do?

Speaking in a quiet voice William said, "I am so sorry for these unfortunate events. I can tell you that when the North West Brigade left for The Forks they did not do so with the intention of

murder. But feelings in the Company run high."
He went on to say that when Miles Macdonell
proclaimed that no pemmican could be taken
from the area, the Nor'Westers believed it was a
direct insult to them. They believed that Lord
Selkirk's settlement was established by the Hudson's
Bay Company to put them out of business.
And then they encouraged the Métis to see themselves
as a separate nation and told them that
their entire way of life was about to be destroyed
by our settlement. "This is not an excuse for the
violence," he said, "but I offer you this as an
explanation so you can better understand that all
North West Company people, all Métis people,
are not violent. I myself do not know what to do.
It is my own Company that has killed my father,
and yet I am still contracted to work for them."

Father put his hand on William's shoulder.
"You have no choice but to adhere to a contract,"
Father said. "But just like Kate, you are welcome
with us." He paused. "Unfortunately I do not
know where we will be. At this point it looks likely
that we will be returning to Scotland. But Kate
will write you and let you know where we are."

William grasped Father's hand in his and
shook it warmly. "Thank you," he said, "you are
very kind. My father was a good man, but never

recovered after the death of my mother, and I am afraid life has been difficult for Kate. She has been too long kept from company and has had few that she could call friend. But I see that you have taken her in and shown her kindness, and am sure God will bless you for your acts."

Suddenly, dear diary, I saw Kate in such a different light. White Loon was no doubt correct in that Kate was perhaps trying to behave, or was behaving, as an annoying little sister. She had no skills at making friends since her father had kept her separated from people all these years, and she must have tried to ingratiate herself with me in the only way she knew how — in a way that would not hurt her pride. Her cheeks grew quite red as her brother talked and she did not contradict him, so I can only assume that what he said was correct. It also occurred to me how fortunate we were that Father decided to come out of his grief. It even seemed to me that perhaps White Loon was to be thanked, not censured.

William was then ordered to help with Mr. McLeod's search, so he took our leave and went to his work. The men of our party were all questioned. Some were even forced to empty their pockets and had to allow their clothes to be searched.

We ate pemmican that night, and stayed the entire next day. Although there was little left to be searched, the Nor'Westers did search all over again.

William spent evenings with us by the fire. And then we saw an entirely new Kate, who seemed like a different person in his presence. He told stories of their home in the Highlands. Kate shared her memories, we added ours. We sang songs from the Highlands, and it turns out that Kate and William have beautiful clear voices, just like songbirds.

June 27

We took our leave this morning and Kate wept as she waved good-bye to her brother. John Pritchard was arrested by the North West Company, as was another fellow. They were to be taken to Fort William. Archibald McLeod then said that if we ever returned to The Forks we would all be subject to the "penalty of death." Murder, I say.

As we got back on the boat and rowed away, Father looked at White Loon. She nodded and pulled a packet from beneath her dress.

"The letters?" I breathed.

"Yes," said Father.

I looked at White Loon in wonder. And now I vow never to think badly of her again. Had she been caught she certainly would have been arrested, perhaps worse. But she was so calm you never would have thought she was hiding important evidence.

Another thought occurred to me as well. White Loon had left her own family behind without a tear, although it must have been wrenching for her.

June 28

We travel on Lake Winnipeg to Jack River House. We are hungry, tired, dispirited.

July 3

Terrible thunderstorms today. Had to make camp.

Kate is like a different person. She sits quietly, has not made a nasty remark all day, smiles occasionally, and even joins in the conversation. It is a transformation I would not have credited even weeks earlier.

July 7

Dreadful weather. We cannot go into the open lake with our boats, as the winds are too strong. It is a tiring and long process to travel so near the banks where we cannot use the gusts of wind to push us ahead. The clouds hover above us and lightning crashes around us. Last night a tree right beside our tent was split in two and set on fire. Frantically we pulled our tent down and moved away from the fire, all the while being drenched by a mixture of hail and pelting rain. It was a miserable night.

On the way south, last fall, we faced the difficulties with more courage because we were so full of hope and excitement for the future. But now these hardships are more difficult to tolerate and I find myself sunk in a black humour most of the time. Only White Loon seems to have retained her equanimity.

Tonight it is calm for the moment, but the clouds refuse to go away. Even now I can hear thunder rumbling in the distance. Since Robbie's Indian friends are no longer here he spends more time with Peter. They are, at the moment, collecting small rocks from each spot where we camp, hoping to bring them back to Scotland.

They call it their Rupert's Land rock collection. Alice comes to our tent whenever possible, and although she does visit with me and Kate, she spends even more time chatting with James. She praised his artistic abilities so strongly that he promised to make her a necklace. She blushed and thanked him and now James, too, is collecting rocks, and busy on his new design. I think we are all trying to keep busy in some way or another, so as not to think about the dreadful events of the past few weeks. Or about our future.

I never had a chance to make myself that skirt out of the hide I was given by Leaf Bud, but now in the evenings White Loon is helping me. It should be finished soon. Father and the other men often meet and talk after camp is set up about what to do once we get to Jack River.

July 15

We make slow progress. I have not been writing because there is little to report and I am working with White Loon on my skirt, which is now almost finished. And just in time, as my other one is literally in tatters. I could, of course, wear one of Mother's dresses that I have made over for myself, but they are delicate and would last only a matter of days in this difficult and rough environment. Also, Father was unable to take all of our clothes. It was the same for the other settlers, so almost all of the women and children are wearing clothes that have practically turned into shreds. We are hoping that when we arrive at Jack River we will be able to buy material.

July 25

We are almost there. We arrived this afternoon at Playgreen Lake, a most beautiful spot. Actually we passed through here on our way to Red River, but the leaves were already off the trees by then, although I remember the tall and magnificent spruce, tamarack and jack pine. There are also birch, poplars and willows that we are very familiar with from the Red River. Everywhere wild flowers are in bloom — blues and bright yellows surround brilliant orange-coloured tiger lilies, and all are set off by the unusual bright orange moss growing on the rocks.

July 26

We have set up camp on the bank of Jack River. Jack River House is on an island only a short row away. Sheriff McDonell went there directly with

Father, who carried the letters saved from the settlement. They returned with frying pans and kettles, blankets, flour, some oil, pemmican and some fresh fish. They also brought twine to make fishing nets. The Factor in charge of the Hudson Bay Post at Jack River is called Bird, James Bird. The big news is that he does not see any prospect at all of our returning to Scotland in the near future! He says that there are no boats travelling back and that we must consider that not only will we be staying this winter, but that we may be here for an entire year before a boat is to be found to return us to our homeland. Although the other settlers seemed distressed by this news, Father is hopeful. He feels that this will give Lord Selkirk time to place us back in the Red River Settlement. Of course, I believe Father to be the most sensible of all men, and would like to believe that he is correct, but I fear that he is only fooling himself.

The first order of business, he says, is to build little cabins for the winter, as we certainly do not want to spend it in tents. First thing tomorrow we begin that job.

August 6

We have built a fairly cosy little hut. We have filled up the holes in between the wood with mud and moss. The roof is made of double layers of poles and is covered with double layers of spruce bark. Father made two sets of bunk beds, one for me and Kate, the other for Robbie and James.

I don't think I understood properly anything about our coming to this New World. Often at night Father and the others, both men and women, gather round the campfire to talk. They are trying to understand what has gone wrong with all our plans, and I listen closely. I am not sure if this is correct, but this is what I understand so far: The Hudson's Bay Company gave Lord Selkirk a grant of this land. Everyone seems to agree that Lord Selkirk had only good intentions, even idealistic intentions, for the settlement. But Father thinks that the Hudson's Bay Company must have had quite different reasons for giving Lord Selkirk the land than he had for wanting it. At one point Father said, "They probably understood that if we settled there we could easily supply the fur traders with food that we ourselves grew, and eventually that would make the Company stronger than the North West Company."

He went on to say that no one had thought about

the new race of people coming from the marriage between Indian and French, creating a people who want to be known as a new people and new nation, the Métis. And the Métis see us settlers as a threat to their way of life. After all, those Métis who do not work for one of the trading companies live from the buffalo, and how can they hunt buffalo if the land is cultivated and the buffalo are driven away? And the settlers are an obvious threat to those who work for the North West Company, because the Nor'Westers have been forbidden to take pemmican from the area, so that there will be enough for the settlers. In a way, then, the settlers are simply pawns between the Hudson's Bay Company and the North West Company.

"Colin Robertson understood this perfectly," Father said, "and therefore understood the danger that we were in, whereas Governor Semple seemed to have no idea of the true danger. His ignorance helped him and those poor unfortunates walk straight into danger."

At that point a number of the women who had lost their husbands at Seven Oaks began to cry. As did Kate.

"No doubt all those lives could have been saved if they had stayed in the protection of the Fort, or at least taken the big gun with them and been prepared to fire. We thought we'd come to this land to be free," Father said, "but we are still being used by those higher than us."

August 10

Have had little time to write as every night we spend sewing and mending socks and underclothes, which are in a sorry state.

August 11

Alice, Kate and I were out today picking wild strawberries. We found some wonderful patches. And we also encountered the Cree women who are camped nearby. They did not speak to us at first, but I knew from meeting with White Loon's people that that was not because they were necessarily unfriendly, it was just their way. I would be tempted to call them shy, but I have begun to realize that just because people behave differently than me doesn't mean I understand why they do so. If it were somebody from the Highlands and they were quiet, I would assume that they were shy or unfriendly, but perhaps this is just the way the Cree women are. At any rate we made an effort to be friendly, and they responded right away. They were wonderful about sharing the patches with us. They could, of course, have shooed us away, but it did not seem that even occurred to them.

A couple of them were girls our age, and they told me they were from the Swampy Cree band. One is named Bends Fingers. She is tall and beautiful. She showed us that she can bend her fingers all the way back because she is double-jointed. One of the other girls is called Sings Well and the third is called Whose Face Shows Her Moods. I couldn't help but wonder at such interesting names, and asked them how they got them. It turns out it is not the least bit the same as how we get our names, with our mother and father telling us what it is. First it seems that there is a ceremony within days of the child being born. In this ceremony a group of birth songs are sung to the child by the father or by the shaman, before a gathering of family and guests. The name can be based on physical characteristics or the personality of the child, or some event that might have happened to a child, or some animal the child is akin to, or even some war, or an event such as the weather. Often children change their names if they feel that the name they have no longer suits them. And then they end up with names like Bends Fingers! I wonder if I were to change my name, what I would change it to? Would it still be Wishes To Be A Lady or something else altogether?

When we returned with our strawberries White
Loon showed us how to press them into cakes. We
then left them out to dry so they could be put away
for the winter.

August 15

Today we went berry picking again, this time looking for black currants. Bends Fingers came to get us
and showed us where the best patches were. She can
move and twist herself into the most amazing posi-
tions and she seems to be double-jointed all over.
Kate seems to have nothing good to say to her and
in private only makes fun of her. In fact Kate seems
to have reverted to her old self, and I wonder if the
gentle and reasoned person we saw when her brother was here was only a mirage. White Loon says she
is jealous of my new friends. What a prickly girl she
is!

August 28

We have been in the New Land for one year. To
avoid despair and despondency Father and Jasper
McKay organized a party. We danced for hours. It
was a good thing because otherwise we would have
been filled with gloom, thinking how we have come
to such a pass.

September 1

Big news! BIG NEWS!

A letter has arrived from Colin Robertson today saying that Lord Selkirk will make sure that we are able to return to The Forks.

I dare not believe that what the letter says is true. I think that perhaps our dreams were destroyed at Frog Plain. (Speaking of dreams, I have suffered the most terrible nightmares since that dreadful day.)

September 8

White Loon works all day. She is making us winter jackets from caribou skins she has managed to obtain from the Indian women by trading some of our pots.

Kate and I are going out in a boat with Bends Fingers to help harvest wild rice.

September 9

Today was tremendous fun. I love the Indian way of life. But I do not understand why that is so. It is nothing like the ladylike life I envisioned for myself, sitting pouring tea and eating scones with cream. But it was so beautiful to drift out into the water in a canoe, passing through the tall grass, the warm sun streaming down. The mosquitoes are almost gone, now that it is well into September. The rocks around us were covered in bright orange moss. The birds were singing. My job was to catch the long stems of rice and shake them over the boat so that the kernels dropped into the bottom. Bends Fingers has promised that we can help harvest the rice with them over the next few days and that then we shall have a part of it. Won't White Loon be proud of us when we come home with rice for the winter? I will be telling her none of this as I want it to be a surprise.

September 10

Today Bends Fingers fetched us to the Indian camp and we watched as they heated the rice kernels over a large fire. Then the kernels were thrown into a big pit in the ground. Bends Fingers' brother, Broken Nose, proceeded to jump up and down in the hole. I was horrified at first, thinking that he was being a bad boy and destroying the rice. In fact, that is the way they separate the husks from the kernels.

September 11

Bends Fingers ran into our cabin calling out to us, "Wind, wind, follow me, follow me."

Kate had gone to the river to help White Loon with the laundry and I had stayed to clean fish for our dinner.

I ran to Alice's cabin and fetched her. Then we hurried after Bends Fingers to their encampment, which is through a beautiful stand of tall pine trees and low bushes. All the women and girls from the camp were gathered in a treeless space near the tipis. They were each holding a large flat piece of birchbark. Then one of the women came by with a birchbark basket. Out of this basket she took handfuls of the rice and the husks and put them on the birchbark pieces. The women and girls began to throw the rice and husks into the air. The husks blew away in the wind and only the rice remained! Soon we were being taught how to do it as well, and although sometimes I dropped some of the rice, I quickly learned. We did this all afternoon until my arms felt that they were going to fall off, but in the end I was given an entire basket full of rice to take home. Both White Loon and Father were very proud of me and delighted with my acquisition.

September 20

Is it nine days since I last wrote in your pages? The time has passed so quickly and so pleasantly that there have even been a few nights when I have not suddenly wakened, gasping for breath, reliving over and over that terrible day at Frog Plain. We have been berry picking daily and we eat well, as the fish are abundant.

Unfortunately everyone's clothes are in tatters, and although White Loon has done some good trading and has managed to get us some excellent skins, Father still needed to go to the Company store for material. Everything that we must buy from the store puts us further into debt with the Company. This debt was to be paid off by our working the land for them and paying them by supplying them with food. But now that we are to go back to the Highlands how will we ever pay them back? I know this weighs heavily on Father and on James.

September 22

Robbie's birthday is tomorrow. We were unable to celebrate last year as we were on that difficult long trip from York Factory. He does nothing but grow, so for my present I am making him a new pair of moccasins. Father has managed to get flour and a small bit of sugar from the Company and I will also make a cake. James is fashioning him a bracelet. Father and White Loon will not say what their present will be.

September 23

We had a party for Robbie today and all his friends from the settlement came, as did the Indian boys. They played games all afternoon. White Loon and Father gave Robbie his very own bow and arrow. He was so thrilled that I think he could not wait for the games to be over so he could go and practise. Peter is jealous and is now begging his parents for one as well so he can go hunting with Robbie.

September 30

It has become bitterly cold. I think it will snow soon.

October 1

It snowed today and the wind blew cold. I cannot say I am looking forward to a long bitter winter. It would not be so difficult if we knew that we could go back to The Forks in the spring. But the spring will bring only more waiting until a ship can take us home again. And then what? Our old home might now be overrun by sheep so that we cannot farm. Will we end up in the slums of Glasgow like all the rest of the people thrown off the land?

October 4

I have decided to put on a theatrical for the entire group of settlers. I have been trying to think how we can keep occupied on these long nights. It seems to me that we can devise a play and practise it. Already James, Alice, Kate, Robbie, Peter and Bends Fingers have said they wish to participate. We have all decided that we shall try to tell the story of our last year using humour and song. If we can do a good job this theatrical can be played for generations to come to tell our story. I know that Mother would be pleased as it is another way to develop my writing skills, and a more public way, since this diary is to be read by no one but myself.

October 6

Kate wishes to represent the North West Company in the story. She says her brother told her many details that we may not know about the Company and that the Company is not all bad. As for me, I think it delightfully appropriate that Kate play the villain.

The weather has warmed a bit.

October 15

I am too busy writing our theatrical to also write in your pages every night. Also I am beginning to be concerned because I notice that I am coming to the end of this diary. Father has tried to find one for me at the Company store but there are none.

October 16

The theatrical has been put aside for the moment. We must all help to bring in the fish. It is at this time of year that the whitefish move out of the deep waters where they dwell, to spawn closer to shore. Father and the other men have made small birchbark canoes, copying the canoes of the Swampy Cree. They use cedar for the frame and the ribs. Then they select a birch tree and peel its bark off in one piece with a sharp knife. You have to be very careful not to break the bark in any spot. Then they take the fibres of roots of the spruce and they soak them in water; when they're soft they rub them until they're so flexible they can use them just like thread to tie the canoe together. This took them a few days but finally we had a lovely little canoe. One drawback — they are very light and easy to tip, nothing at all like the York boats that we travelled on more recently.

I'm afraid that a couple of times James was so busy making a joke that he was not careful and he tipped the canoe. The experience was extremely unpleasant I am sure as the water has turned cold.

October 25

Thousands and thousands of fish have been caught. Father says the number is well over ten thousand. We work day and night gutting them, cleaning them and drying them for the winter. Naturally we're eating fish every night. I am fortunate that I like fish, but Robbie cannot bear even the smell of it. Father insists that he eat and says that there's no possibility of such preferences under these circumstances. Robbie screws up his face and pushes the fish around his plate. Father can say what he likes — Robbie is far too stubborn to listen. I try to make sure that he always has bannock and I have seen White Loon giving him berries numerous times. Often he goes and eats at the Indian camp with his friends, where he is much happier eating freshly killed meat.

October 26

The men spent today mending the canoes so they could go out fishing again. First they sew up the breaks with spruce thread, as the Indians showed them. Then they heat the gum from the spruce tree and pour that into the cracks in the canoe. When it hardens in the cold water it appears to make a watertight seal. Again I am impressed by these so-called savages. Did I say savages? It seems that I can no longer look at them that way.

November 10

Snow covers the ground. The fishing is over. And we are back to our theatrical.

November 23

I am running out of pages in this diary. I will only be able to write short passages from now on.

November 29

We will present our theatrical on Hogmanay.
Kate continues to surprise me. She has a flair for
the dramatic and is the best player we have. James
is also very good, and much to Alice's dismay,
James and Kate spend all their free time rehears-
ing. Kate's personality seems to undergo a
change at these times, just as it did when her
brother was here. When she is occupied with
something that she is good at, her mood lightens,
she smiles and rarely utters a cross or nasty word.
I do not know what to make of her still. Alice,
unfortunately, has decided that Kate is dissem-
bling in order to find favour with James, and has
begun to hate her. I think it is unfortunate
because Alice is such a mild soul who has a kind
word for everyone, but Kate is bringing out the
worst in her. In the meantime, as writer and
director of the theatrical I must mediate between
them, and often find myself caught between my
brother, Kate and Alice. Certainly it has given us
a diversion, but I could have wished for a more
relaxed diversion than this!

I vowed to write only short passages and see
how I have blathered on.

December 8

The weather is so bitterly cold it has become almost unbearable. The thermometer is registering at minus thirty-five degrees. When I go outside my nostrils stick together as I breathe, a most unpleasant sensation. James must be covered up and I have sewn him a hood that covers his face and ears, leaving only his eyes and mouth free, otherwise he would freeze his skin again. Robbie and his friends have built a snow fort and they meet there daily. The cold doesn't seem to bother them.

December 14

White Loon is helping me make new rabbit mittens for everyone as Handsel Monday presents. She set out traps and we have been tending them with great success. An extra benefit is delicious rabbit stew.

January 1, 1817

Our theatrical was a triumph. Only a couple of pages left so I cannot give details, but Kate was magnificent. She is the queen of the settlers for the moment, and even when she is not immersed in this activity she appears to be a new person —

not soft, but with a cutting sense of humour that does not hurt others, but is still sharp and keen.

All the settlers celebrated together, but no one knows what the New Year will bring. I try not to be depressed by our prospects but it isn't easy. Kate wants to do another theatrical about life in the Highlands. We start on it tomorrow. I am helping daily in the school that has been set up for the children.

February 19

I miss writing in these pages. I have only a few pages left and have been saving them for the day when we leave this land. Robbie has been very ill, but White Loon has nursed him back to health using Indian remedies. It seems she has managed to save both me and my brother, so I must note that Father made a good and wise choice. And I even think that, Mother, you are probably thankful that White Loon has protected your children so well.

March 3

A messenger has arrived with news so unexpected and so marvellous I have to try to stop my hand from trembling as I write. Lord Selkirk was in Montreal when he heard of our trials. He immediately hired a band of soldiers who had fought in the War of 1812. They proceeded directly to Fort William, where they took the North West Company fort from them in the dead of night. Lord Selkirk sent Miles Macdonell ahead with the soldiers. They captured Fort Daer in Pembina and then recaptured Fort Douglas! Father and many of the other men are to go back to The Forks before the ice breaks up so they can plant crops in the spring, and we are to join them in the summer when all will be made ready for us.

Father was right not to give up hope. I did not realize how deeply my feelings went until I heard this news. I realize that I have fallen in love with this land.

I hate to leave my new friends behind, Bends Fingers, Sings Well and Whose Face Shows Her Moods. But they say we will meet again and I look forward to seeing my other Indian friends in The Forks again. It seems that my fears about becoming like the savages has completely disappeared. Because they are not savages at all, but good people who have different ways than us. And who knows, soon I might have a little half-Indian brother or sister.

Dear Mother, I pray that your vision for us will yet come true. We will live free in this new land.

June 19

We are back at The Forks!

July 18

Dear diary, dear Mother, this will be my last entry. But with what hope I leave your precious pages. Today Lord Selkirk met with us on Frog Plain, the site of our tragedy, and made us a gift of the land and wiped clean our debt. He is also giving us land for a school and a church. I saw Father shed a tear — in fact, there was not a dry eye to be seen.

Lord Selkirk is to make a treaty with Chief Peguis and the Indian bands and both "chiefs" are very proud.

It is a strange thing. I no longer care about being a fine lady. I believe that Mother was right. God is good, kind and loving. I wish for nothing but to be as good a woman as Mother and White Loon. And Father promises me that he will order me another diary from England as soon as possible.

So farewell for now.

Mother, give us your blessing.

Epilogue

Isobel and her family had high hopes when they returned to The Forks. And they did spend a lovely summer. The weather was fine and the crops flourished. As long as they could get their crop in they would be able to stay in their homes for the winter. But nature played them a nasty trick. An early frost decimated the crop and any grain that was saved had to be used for seed. They were forced to leave the colony and winter in Pembina at Fort Daer, where they encountered one of the worst winters on record.

It didn't get much easier. The next summer, grasshoppers descended on the Red River area, 3 inches deep in some places. And the next year, because of the eggs the grasshoppers left behind, there was another wave, which left only enough grass for hay. Isobel had to crawl on her hands and knees, along with the other settlers, just to salvage any seed they could for the next season. In fact, they ended up going south every winter for years to come.

The settlers remained caught in the conflict

between the two fur trading companies. The rivalry was the cause of sometimes vicious fighting between the two, although often the "battles" were fought not physically but financially. Each tried to set lower barter rates with the Indians to gain more business, a practice that actually cost them more money and gave them lower profits. The British government was pressing for there to be just one trading company, with the exclusive right to trade in furs throughout the west — all the way to the Pacific Ocean. With profits threatened and the government pressing for amalgamation, the two fur trading companies eventually merged into The Hudson's Bay Company in 1821. For the Selkirk settlers the union was a positive turn of events. They had enough trouble battling nature.

Isobel became very close to White Loon and to White Loon's family. She had three siblings born over the next five years, and it took all her time and strength to help care for them and do the other work expected of the women: cooking, cleaning, sewing and tending the garden.

When Isobel was eighteen and her brother James was twenty-one, he married Kate. They had a stormy marriage, but loved each other. Kate and Isobel grew closer over the years, and by the time they were in their twenties they were fast friends. Alice was broken-hearted, but not for long. She was wooed by another boy in the settlement and they married and were very happy, having twelve children.

The family worked hard and the colonists became a tightly knit community. In 1825 their fortitude was tested again. Isobel was twenty-two by then. Both her brothers were married, as were all her friends, but she was too busy with the younger children to think about a beau. At least that is what she always said. That winter there was a terrible blizzard and the settlers were trapped in between The Forks and Pembina. Thirty-three settlers died that winter, including James's newborn son. James and Kate later had three girls who survived, but they always mourned their lost son, William.

By May 3, 1826, water levels were unusually high. By May 5, after days of cold and rainy weather, the Red River overflowed its banks. Hudson's Bay Company officials helped the settlers move to higher ground at Stony Mountain and Bird's Hill. Forty-seven houses were destroyed by the flood, including Isobel's family's house.

But there is a saying that every cloud has a silver lining, and there certainly was one in this case. One of the young men who helped the settlers was a fellow who had just arrived from Scotland. The younger son of an earl, just as Lord Selkirk had been, he fell in love with Isobel on the spot and set about wooing her. Although she had long since ceased to care about being a lady, she saw in this young man many of her father's qualities. Robert was caring, considerate, smart and very funny. And he was always there to help during the next difficult months after the settlers returned to find total and complete devastation. And to add to the settlers' misery, because of all the rain, the mosquitoes were as bad as any Biblical plague. In all, 250 people, half the settlement's population, left after the flood, looking for a safer, less difficult place to live. All the hardy Selkirk Settlers stayed. And that fall Isobel married.

Robert unexpectedly inherited money from his mother two years later. He built Isobel a grand home on the banks of the Red River. She had servants and all she had once dreamed of, but she no longer cared much about such things. She spent most of her time helping others, and began some of the earliest charities in the town that, by 1866, was called Winnipeg.

Isobel and Robert had six healthy children — four boys and two girls. They lost the seventh in childbirth.

Isobel died an old woman in the year 1883. About that same time the last remaining buffalo on the prairie was sighted, and the Cree hunting parties were starving to death. That way of life was forever over.

Historical Note

It was the battle of Culloden in 1746 that changed life on the Scottish Highlands forever. Bonnie Prince Charlie, grandson of King James II, tried to overthrow King George II of England, but failed. Prince Charlie, "King o' the Highland Hearts," had 30,000 clansmen at his side when he failed in this attempt. When it was over, a stroke of a pen in England banned all of the clans in Scotland. Life would never be the same.

Before this catastrophe each man in each clan owned his own land and elected a chief as an overlord. They raised black, long-haired cattle and grew their own grain, which they ground at a common mill. When the clans were banned, property was taken away from the individuals and given to the chieftains. At first this made little difference, as the old chieftains honoured the old practices. But when a new generation of chieftains — who were educated in England — took control, life changed. Former property owners became nothing more than tenants who had to pay rent to the lords. These proud people would naturally be attracted to a life that promised them independence once again. In addition, many of the landlords, finding that they made more money letting sheep graze their land than having crofters farm it, began to turn the people off the land — a dark time in Scottish history later known as the Clearances.

In 1670 Charles II of England, prompted by the western explorations of voyageurs such as Pierre-Esprit Radisson and Médard Chouart Des Groseilliers, had granted a charter to his cousin, Prince Rupert, and to the "Governor and Company of Adventurers Trading in Hudson's Bay." There already existed an established fur trade business in the New World, but it operated out of Montreal. The Hudson's Bay Company would take the furs it had collected and ship them directly to Europe via Hudson Bay, bypassing the Montreal traders such as the North West Company.

Though it may be difficult to imagine an entire company existing to trade in furs, one was needed to supply the huge appetite in Europe for the felt hats made from beaver fur. And this was not a passing fashion. The style of one's beaver hat

160

indicated social status, and over half a million beaver pelts were auctioned off in London during the Company's most active years. Though much of the Hudson's Bay Company's original trading was from the shores of Hudson Bay itself, it was eventually forced to move farther inland to meet the challenge of the North West Company. Fur traders canoed, portaged and trekked through the 3 million square miles (almost 8 million square kilometres) of territory granted to the Company — all the lands of not only Hudson Bay, but the rivers that drained into it. Some of those rivers originated as far west as the foothills of the Rocky Mountains, creating a territory almost unimaginably vast.

The fact that there were traders, factors and numerous posts belonging to the Hudson's Bay Company created a sort of northern perimeter in the face of American colonizers who might otherwise have expanded farther northward. The trading posts often formed the centre of settlements built around them, and some of these key posts, such as Fort Garry (Winnipeg) and Fort Edmonton, eventually became some of Canada's most important cities. In many ways, the history of the Hudson's Bay Company is inseparable from the history of Canada.

In 1810 Lord Selkirk proposed to the Company that it grant him land for a settlement within their territory. Selkirk was looking for a place to relocate the thousands of Scottish Highlanders being driven off their land by the Clearances. The Company obliged by granting him 116,000 square miles of Hudson Bay Company territory (300,000 square kilometres) — a massive tract of land that covered much of present-day southern Manitoba and some of North Dakota and Minnesota, as well as eastern Saskatchewan and even a small part of northern Ontario. The land grant, called Assiniboia, came with one stipulation: this colony would furnish the Hudson's Bay Company with labourers.

As soon as they heard of this deal, the rival North West Company of Montreal launched a negative press campaign against the colony. Scottish newspapers were full of horror stories about the dreadful conditions that would await the settlers upon their arrival in the new land. Nevertheless Lord Selkirk's agents went to Ireland and Scotland to engage servants for the Company and general labourers for the colony. They found many willing to join. The settlers would be paid

£20 a year by the Company and would receive 100 acres of land (about 40 hectares) free of charge, after they had helped build up a colony.

Miles Macdonell was appointed the first Governor of the new colony. He travelled to York Factory on Hudson Bay in mid-July of 1811, with a party of labourers who were promised 20 acres of land for their work. They were to prepare for the actual settlers' arrival the following year. On October 27, 1812, the first group of settlers arrived at Red River. They immediately had to travel south to Pembina, as this was where the buffalo went in the winter, and without other food supplies they needed buffalo meat in order to survive until they could plant crops in the spring.

In the spring of 1813 the settlers returned to farm near Fort Douglas at the forks of the Red and Assiniboine rivers — The Forks, the site Macdonell had chosen for the new colony. They built log huts that fronted on the Red River. They planted crops, but by the fall of 1813 it was obvious that the colony was in trouble. The crops they had planted — winter and spring wheat, peas, hemp, English barley, rye, corn — all failed. The only crop that survived was the potatoes. The settlers were forced again to spend the winter in Pembina.

A second group of settlers arrived in the new land in the fall of 1813. After typhoid broke out on their ship the captain was so anxious to get rid of his passengers that he dropped them on the banks of the Churchill River, even farther north than York Factory. It was already late in September so there was nothing to do but stay put. They had to build huts, but were so weak it took a long time to get them finished. The only supplies available were from York Factory, too far away, and officials there didn't want to send any stores to the settlers. The men vowed that they would not be discouraged, however. The women, too, refused to give in to the weather and the lack of food, and somehow they survived. In April they walked all the way to York Factory, a trek of 150 miles (240 kilometres) that took them thirteen days. The men went ahead with sledges and cut a path for the women because there was still snow covering the ground.

In late June of 1814 they arrived at The Forks. There Governor Miles Macdonell supervised the building of a fine Government House, which he called Fort Douglas after Thomas Douglas, Lord

Selkirk. The settlers' hopes were high, but they were caught between several conflicting interests. The Red River colony was on land that the Métis had long occupied, as well as being in the path of the Nor'Westers' route to the west. Another sore point was scarcity of food: the settlers needed pemmican to survive — pemmican that the Nor'Westers also needed to carry on their long journeys into the interior. Relations between the two companies — already strained — grew increasingly tense during the late eighteenth and early nineteenth centuries.

In January of 1814 Miles Macdonell had issued the Pemmican Proclamation, declaring that the Nor'Westers could not take pemmican out of Assiniboia. Macdonell also seized the pemmican at Fort Gibraltar, the North West post close to Fort Douglas, and gave it to the settlers so they were able to winter at Fort Douglas instead of travelling all the way to south Pembina. But the settlers did not realize that they had a fox amongst the chickens. A former army officer (and later a partner in the North West Company), Duncan Cameron would dress up in his military finest and invite the settlers for dinner. He would tell them that they were in danger from the

Indians, but if they went to Upper Canada they would be given free land and free transport — even free food for a year. He even promised to pay the wages Lord Selkirk might owe them. Cameron was one of them, a Scot, so the settlers believed him.

Miles Macdonell was arrested for taking the Nor'Westers' pemmican. Shortly after, many settlers accepted Cameron's offer to leave for Upper Canada. When they had left, the Nor'Westers burned their homes and the crops and drove off their animals. The few settlers who refused to leave were forced to flee to Jack River at the north end of Lake Winnipeg. It is then that the third group of settlers arrived, the group that Isobel's story is about. They too were plagued with both flooding and harsh winters, yet many managed to survive.

Thomas Douglas, Lord Selkirk, died in April of 1820, his fortunes much diminished. He had been involved in lengthy legal battles relating to his taking of Fort William from the North West Company in the spring of 1817, when he had travelled from Montreal to The Forks to help the settlers after receiving news of the battle of Seven Oaks.

On May 4, 1836, Lord Selkirk's heirs sold Assiniboia back to the Hudson's Bay Company for £84,000 worth of Hudson's Bay Company stock. A new fort, Upper Fort Garry, was built at The Forks at the site of the old Fort Gibraltar. And the city of Winnipeg has grown up around it.

Landing of the Selkirk Settlers. Red River, 1812

Lord Selkirk sent over several groups of settlers from Scotland to farm land in the Red River valley. This painting shows the arrival of the first wave of settlers in 1812.

Thomas Douglas, Lord Selkirk, had earlier placed Scottish settlers in both Upper Canada and Prince Edward Island, before going ahead with settlements in the Red River area.

Saulteaux Chief Peguis and his people were very helpful to the Red River settlers.

Miles Macdonell, first governor of the Red River settlement, aggravated relations between the Hudson's Bay and North West companies with his Pemmican Proclamation.

Elaborate ceremonies normally preceded the actual trading of furs at Hudson's Bay Company posts such as York Factory.

This sketch of Fort Douglas, at The Forks, is from a copy of a sketch made by Lord Selkirk himself.

Winter fishing on the ice where the Red and Assiniboine rivers meet. Fort Gibraltar is shown at the left, with Fort Douglas across the river, at the right.

A Red River cart train meets a group of York boats. The York boats were so called because they were a main form of transportation between York Factory and posts farther south.

Fur traders often had to portage their canoes both to travel inland to collect furs and to bring them back to the post.

A Red River cart travelling past a settler's homestead in Manitoba.

The drama of a buffalo hunt, using a pound to pen the huge animals, is shown in this image of an 1820s' hunt.

Governor Semple and other settlers fighting with a group of Métis at the Battle of Seven Oaks.

A view of Forts Pembina and Daer, at Pembina on the Red River, in 1822.

The original Fort Garry was built by the Hudson's Bay Company between 1817 and 1822, at the junction of the Red and Assiniboine rivers. Upper Fort Garry, shown here, was begun in 1835 at a site to the west of the original fort.

The Red Lake Chief, making a Speech to the Governor of the Red River settlement at Fort Douglas in 1823.

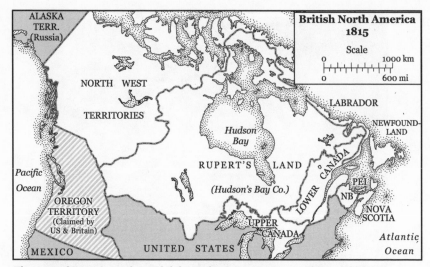

The grant of Rupert's Land provided the Hudson's Bay Company with over 7,770,000 square kilometres of land.

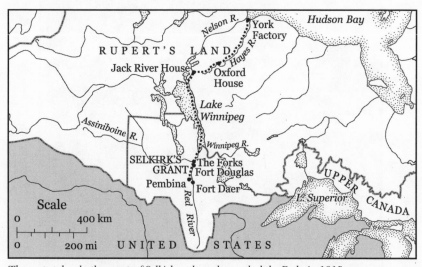

The route taken by the group of Selkirk settlers who reached the Forks in 1815.

Acknowledgments

Grateful acknowledgment is made for permission to reprint the following:

Cover portrait: National Gallery of Scotland, Alexander Ignatius Roche, *Nell*, detail (NG 1733).

Cover background (detail) and page 171 lower: National Archives of Canada, Peter Rindisbacher, *Winter fishing on ice of Assynoibain* [sic] *& Red River*, C-001932.

Ornament: Prairie crocus, Manitoba's provincial flower, Yüksel Hassan.

Page 168: Hudson's Bay Company Archives, Provincial Archives of Manitoba, J.E. Schaflein, *Landing of the Selkirk Settlers, 1812*, HBCA P-388 (N8196). This painting was used as the cover of the Hudson's Bay Company's 1924 calendar.

Page 169 upper: Provincial Archives of Manitoba, *Selkirk, Thomas Douglas (5th Earl) 2*, N8752.

Page 169 lower left: Provincial Archives of Manitoba, Peter Rindisbacher, *Indian [possibly Chief Pequis]* [sic], N3753.

Page 169 lower right: Provincial Archives of Manitoba, *Miles Macdonell 1*, N16074.

Page 170: Hudson's Bay Company Archives, Provincial Archives of Manitoba, Adam Sherriff Scott, *Trading Ceremony at York Factory, 1780's*, HBCA P-420 (N11735). This painting by Adam Sherriff Scott was used as the cover of the Hudson's Bay Company's 1956 calendar

Page 171 upper: Provincial Archives of Manitoba, *Fort Douglas 5*, from a copy of pencil sketch made by Lord Selkirk, 1817, N10109.

Page 172: Glenbow Archives, Calgary, Canada, *Red River cart train*, W.A. Rogers, NA-1406-47.

Page 173: Hudson's Bay Company Archives, Provincial Archives of Manitoba, *At the Portage. Hudson's Bay Company's*

Employés on their annual Expedition, from *Picturesque Canada, Volume 1,* edited by George Monro Grant, published by Belden Bros., Toronto, 1882. HBCA 1987/363-P-28/7 (N13764).

Page 174 upper: *Red River Settler's House and Cart,* National Archives of Canada, William Hind, C-13965.

Page 174 lower: National Archives of Canada, *A Buffalo Pound,* George Back (Engraver: George Finden), C-033615.

Page 175: C.W. Jefferys (1869-1951), *The Fight at Seven Oaks/* Watercolour over pencil on commercial board/35.7 x 47.4 cm (support)/National Archives of Canada, Ottawa (Acc. no. 1972-26-779; repro. no. C-073715). This painting was used as the cover illustration for the Hudson's Bay Company's 1914 calendar.

Page 176 upper: National Archives of Canada, Peter Rindisbacher, *View of the two Company Forts on the level prairie at Pembina on the Red River,* C-1934.

Page 176 lower: National Archives of Canada, *Interior of Fort Garry,* lithograph, C-10531.

Page 177: Toronto Public Library Historical Picture Collection, W. Day, after attributed to H. Jones after Peter Rindisbacher, *The Red Lake Chief, making a Speech to the Governor of Red River at Fort Douglas in 1825,* JRR 2348, Repro number T 15957.

Page 178: Maps by Paul Heersink/Paperglyphs. Map data © 2000 Government of Canada with permission from Natural Resources Canada.

For all my young cousins,
a new generation of hardy Winnipeggers:
Miranda and Hannah Baran
Daniel, Rebecca and Max Asper
Stephen and Jonathan Asper
Sarah and Olivia Asper
(and any new additions yet to come)

I would like to thank the many experts
who helped me with this manuscript:
My researcher, Lewis St. George Stubbs, archival
assistant at the University of Manitoba, was tireless in
his quest for the facts. Dr. Jack Bumsted, Professor of
History at the University of Manitoba, read the
manuscript for accuracy. Anne Morten, Head of
Research and Reference at the Hudson's Bay Company
Archives, was kind enough to answer my questions.
Dr. Bill Waiser of the Department of History,
University of Saskatchewan, read the final version
and made many valuable suggestions. Barbara
Hehner carefully checked a multitude of facts.
My editor, Sandy Bogart Johnston, worked very hard
with me on the manuscript, and I thank her for all
her help. And thank you to Diane Kerner
for her comments as well.

About the Author

Carol Matas is one of Canada's leading writers of historical fiction. She is particularly noted for her books about the Holocaust, such as *Daniel's Story* (shortlisted for the Governor General's Award and winner of the Silver Birch Award), *After the War* and *The Garden* (both winners of the Jewish Book Award), *Lisa,* and *Greater Than Angels.* But she has written books on other historical periods as well, such as *Rebecca* and *The War Within,* contemporary stories like *The Lost Locket* and thrillers such as *Cloning Miranda* and *The Second Clone.* Even fantasies are part of her repertoire.

Carol lives with her family in Winnipeg, so she has a keen appreciation of what the Selkirk Settlers went through in their first years on the prairie, before they were able to settle more permanently and build better shelters for themselves. "I grew up in Manitoba," she says. "As I wrote and researched this story I couldn't help but marvel at the strength and tenacity of the first settlers. The mosquitoes alone would have been enough to send me screaming back to civilization the first chance I had! Sometimes we have eight months of winter, and when it is thirty below, for at least a couple of them you wonder how the settlers managed, some of them like Isobel with nothing at first but a shawl for warmth."

One of Carol's challenges in writing this story was finding where "truth" lay amid the various — and sometimes contradictory — sources of information about the Selkirk Settlers. The Hudson's Bay Company Archives, located in Winnipeg, provided a great wealth of information, including many original sources. However, there were also times when source A would state the facts one way, and source B would state them another way, and Carol would have to sift through the various accounts to arrive at what actually happened to the settlers. Maps, and tracing the route the settlers took, as well as how they travelled, were another challenge. One very positive element came from this though: Carol was able to enjoy the maps her father had acquired over the years as an amateur map collector.

What was it like spending months with Isobel and the other characters in her story? Carol evidently has a fondness for them all. Fondness, and a great respect for the trials they not only endured, but succeeded in meeting with practicality and determination. "As I sit at my desk working on this book on a warm summer day, the birds singing, a breeze blowing in through the window, I say a hearty thank-you to them all. Brave souls."

All rights reserved. Published by Scholastic Canada Ltd.
SCHOLASTIC and DEAR CANADA and logos are trademarks
and/or registered trademarks of Scholastic Inc.

National Library of Canada Cataloguing in Publication Data

Matas, Carol, 1949–
Footsteps in the snow : the Red River diary of Isobel Scott

(Dear Canada)
ISBN 0-439-98835-7

1. Immigrant children – Prairie Provinces – Juvenile fiction.
2. Frontier and pioneer life – Prairie Provinces – Juvenile fiction.
3. Northwest, Canadian – History – To 1870 – Juvenile fiction.
I. Title. II. Series.

PS8576.A7994F66 2002   jC813'.54   C2001-902696-X
PZ7.M423964Fo 2002

6 5   Printed in Canada   04 05

The display type was set in Thomas Paine.
The text was set in New Baskerville.

Printed in Canada
First printing, January 2002

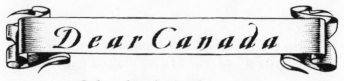

Brothers Far from Home
The World War I Diary of Eliza Bates
by Jean Little

An Ocean Apart
The Gold Mountain Diary of Chin Mei-ling
by Gillian Chan